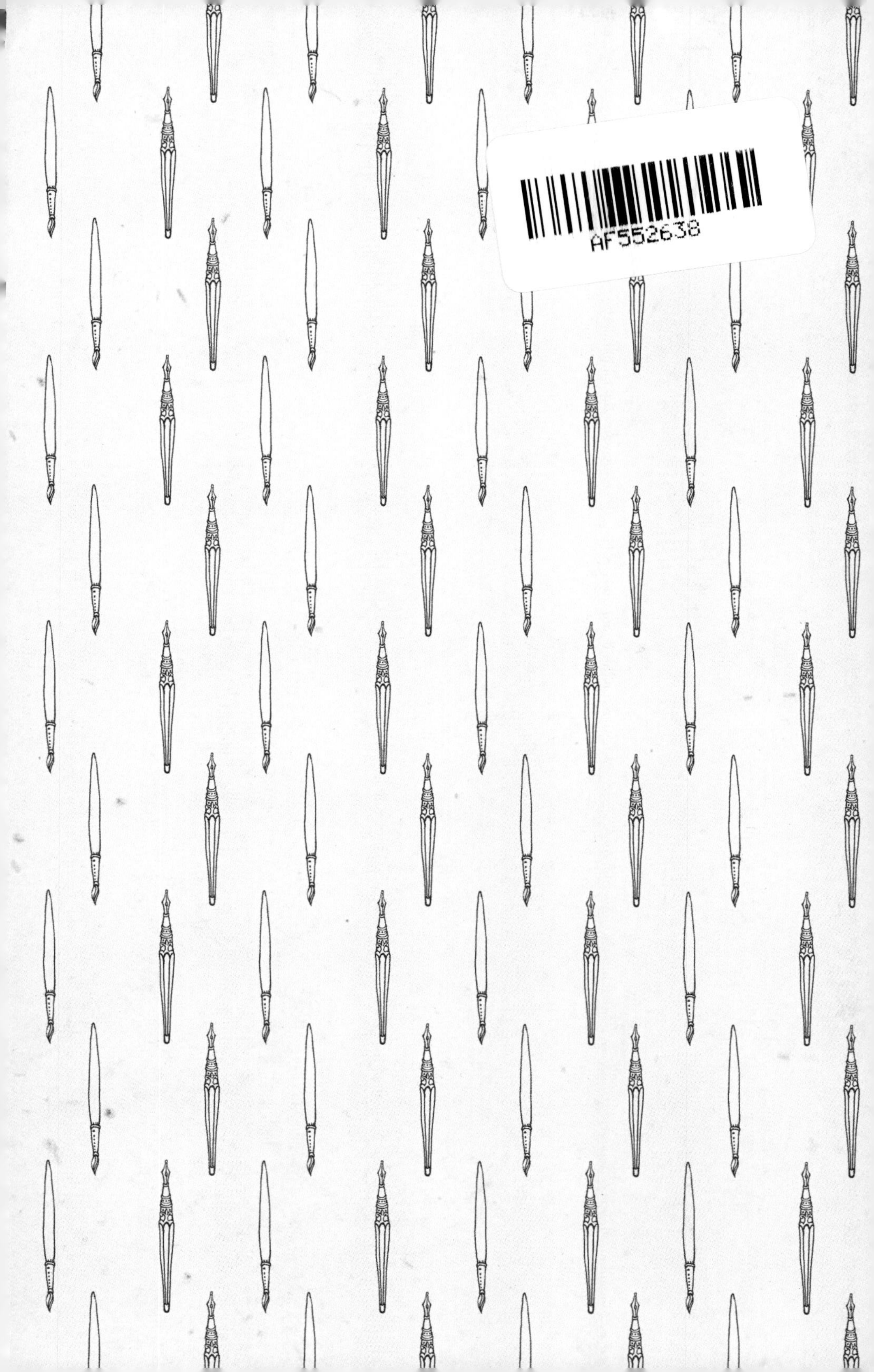
AF552638

INSPIRATIONAL ART & STORIES FOR THE YOUNG MINDS

ARTISTS

Alishka Varde Singh, Devashish Makhija, Bijit Kundu, Late Krsna Ananda, Ruchi Bakshi Sharma, Bimal Poddar, Anoop Patnaik, Kapil Sharma, Kriti Monga, Archan Nair, Rajesh Soni, Allen Shaw, Nitin Patel, Prashant Miranda, Sunaina Sadarangani Gera, Rajashree Basu Kundu, Ashdeen Z. Lilaowala, Anuj Sharma, Rajat Nagpal, Kavita Singh Kale, Pradipta Ray, Prasun Basu, Sucharita Sengupta Suri, Amit Ashar, Priya Kuriyan, Shweta Mohapatra

CURATED & WRITTEN BY

Amit Suri

Wonder House

Copyright © Amit Suri 2020
All Rights Reserved.

Design seekred https://seekred.com

Concept developed by TWAGAA MUMBAI https://twagaa.com

(An imprint of Prakash Books Pvt. Ltd.)

Wonder House Books
Corporate & Editorial Office
113-A, 1st Floor, Ansari Road,
Daryaganj, New Delhi-110002
Tel +91 11 2324 7062-65

© Wonder House 2020
All rights reserved. No part of this book may be reproduced or transmitted in any form by any means, electronic or mechanical, including photocopying and recording, or by any information storage and retrieval system except as may be expressly permitted in writing by the publisher.

ISBN : 9789389567915

Printed in India
Printed 2020

dedicated to

the collective spirit of human creativity

in the past, present and future.

contents

Why WOW...................... 6

	The Art	The Story
Attitude..........................	8	10
Balance...........................	12	14
Curiousity........................	16	18
Diligence.........................	20	22
Empathy..........................	24	26
Freedom..........................	28	30
Goodness.........................	32	34
Honesty..........................	36	38
Integrity.........................	40	42
Joy..................................	44	46
Kindness.........................	48	50
Love..............................	52	54
Modesty..........................	56	58
Naivety..........................	60	62
Om Shanti......................	64	66
Persistence.....................	68	70
Quest.............................	72	74
Respect..........................	76	78
Sincerity.........................	80	82
Trust.............................	84	86
Unique...........................	88	90
Valour............................	92	94
Wisdom..........................	96	98
X - The Unknown..........	100	102
Youth............................	104	106
Zeal..............................	108	110

The WOW People........... 112
More Words of Wonder..... 128
Acknowledgements........... 130
Glossary.......................... 134

why wow?

Some things are destined to be, yet they never happen. Then, there are things that were not meant to be but take birth nevertheless. The *WOW - A to Z* is one such book.

It started with a vague dream—one that I could not recall the next morning. Throughout the day, I tried very hard but, as dreams are, it kept evading me. All that I remembered was that I was reading out a bedtime story on 'honesty' to my children when I gradually slunk into slumber, oblivious to my children's constant nudges to keep me awake.

I witnessed a repeat of this on the next night too. While reading out a story on 'modesty' to my children, I slunk into slumber yet again, and I saw the dream once more. This time, when I woke up, the dream stayed with me for longer—throughout the next day and for many days thereafter.

I was pleased to have captured a few frames of my dream this time. Among the many thoughts, the dream made me wonder how our values shape our whole being—giving our lives a purpose, shaping our behaviour, driving our inspirations, steering our beliefs and the various choices that we make. I drifted into thinking what would it be like if our society attached as much importance to imparting core values as it did to teaching disciplines like mathematics and the sciences. Could values be taught in a structured syllabus, at par with all other subjects that typically formed part of our present academic curriculum? Maybe we should have a degree course in the discipline of 'human values'! Would we then grow to be kinder, more self-aware, instinctively compassionate, abundantly curious and wholly peaceful? Aren't these goals as important to life as the other skills? I mulled over all of this.

However, deeming them philosophical and impractical, I dismissed these thoughts and moved on with my daily routine. But, on yet another night, as I read out one more story to my children, the seeds of *WOW - A to Z* germinated in my mind. I quickly jotted down the first few words on human values that popped into my head. Thereafter, I shortlisted 26 words after searching the internet. The selection was done such that each word started with an alphabet of the English language. Once the list was ready, I contacted 26 creative people who I knew personally or followed online, and requested them to contribute a piece of an artistic expression inspired from the word that I would share with them. Without a doubt, all of us agreed that the impression of an art could help trigger young minds to discover the core human values. We decided to call these '**W**ords **O**f **W**onder'.

Over the next few months, the first draft of the book was compiled with 26 works of art, accompanied by an equal number of inspirational quotes. The book looked beautiful; however, somehow, it felt incomplete. Over time, inspired by the WOW artists and their contributions, I wrote 26 stories and re-designed the book to include works of art, quotations and stories for each of the 26 **W**ords **O**f **W**onder. I am deeply humbled by the contribution made by everyone who participated altruistically in this journey—artists, editors, designers and proofreaders. Isn't that WOW enough!

This book, as you now see it, is a dreamlike journey of people, who in the spirit of creativity, connected over an idea and set out on the search for meaning, sharing with you—the readers, their understanding of a word. Flip this book front to back, or back to front, glean through its pages, savour each word, reflect on a quote, enjoy the art and read the story. Make your way to the very end of the book—with a brief write-up on each artist and their thought process while they were conceptualising the art that accompanies each Word Of Wonder.

With *WOW - A to Z*, we hope to inspire all those who dream, to arouse curiosity and enable everyone to join hands. That is its true purpose—to make sense of the reality based on a dream.

Know more about WOW - A to Z at https://wow.twagaa.com

- Amit Suri
(Mumbai, India)

Attitude

is a little thing that makes a big difference.

Winston Churchill

/ˈatɪtjuːd/ a settled way of thinking or feeling about something

A B C D E F G H I J K L M N O P Q R S T U V W X Y Z

A

ATTITUDE

Maria was the tiny and frail one in her class. She, therefore, always stood first in the queue, sat on the first bench in the classroom, and occupied the first seat in the school bus. Not that she was required to do all of this, but being tiny and frail came with certain 'firsts'.

Still, she was not 'first' always... and often made up the rear in the queue. She ate slowly and was the last to finish meals, she walked ploddingly and was the last to reach the class; and, invariably, she was the last in the athletic races. Being tiny and frail came with certain 'lasts' as well.

The 'lasts', among the list of activities in which she trailed others, had often stung Maria. Fifteen days later, the school would host its yearly Annual Athletics Day, and Maria would hit the tracks again with her tiny feet. But this time, she resolved to do better than what she had done in the earlier editions of the yearly event.

That night, Maria saw the race track in her dreams. There was a tiny sapling on the side of the race track. She dreamt that she was watering that small sapling. Maria saw it gradually bloom into a flower. The flower looked up at her and smiled. At that moment, she woke up. It was five a.m. She put on her trainers and went jogging practicing for the annual race. From then on, she dreamt the same dream every day. Each day, she saw the flower grow a bit more than the previous day. The more the flower bloomed, the stronger was Maria's resolve and she practised hard.

On the big day, the whole class stood at the start line. Maria was as ready as a champion would be. In the cacophony of claps, she could hear stray comments from the audience. Not all of them were kind.

"Isn't she too small?" [*"On your marks!"*]

"A mule amid horses!" [*"Get set!"*]

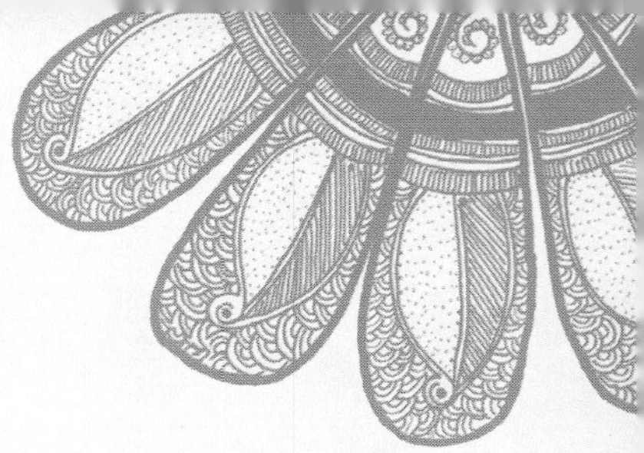

"It seems the last place is already taken." [*"Go!"*]

The race had begun. It was a fine day. The birds were chirping. The clouds drifted smoothly. The sun was bright and warm. The breeze cool and comforting. Although Maria had a late start, she ran like the wild wind. Her feet kissed the ground fleetingly. When the race ended, she had outrun her fancied arch rivals.

While Maria stood smiling with the gold medal dangling around her neck, she remembered the dream. The tiny flower now regaled in full bloom. She heard claps of appreciation from all sides. The principal took over the podium to address the audience and to close the annual event. Her opening lines summed up Maria's achievement: "Attitude is the tiny attribute that makes a big difference."

B

Life is a balance
of holding on and letting go.
Rumi

/ˈbal(ə)ns/ the ability to move or to remain in a position without losing control or falling

A **B** C D E F G H I J K L M N O P Q R S T U V W X Y Z

---

* *To read the poem by Devashish Makhija, flip to page 131*

BALANCE

"I am hungry."

Seema could not turn the boy away. An orphan herself, who had climbed the ladder of social mobility by starting out as a ragpicker, she still remembered the pangs of hunger. Besides, Seema also knew what it felt like being an orphan.

"Come in. Take this."

The boy grabbed the chipped cup and drank the milk in one large swig. Then he devoured pieces of bread and collapsed on the floor in a heap. Seema knew, intuitively, that he had fallen asleep. This was not an emergency. She lifted the boy and placed him on the bed.

Ram, Seema's son, returned from school and found the boy sleeping on his bed. Seema told Ram that the boy was his long-lost brother. Ram was thrilled. He had always wanted sibling company. Ram had a memory of his father sleeping like the boy did now. Seema had told Ram, "Papa went out for work when you were small. He will be back after a few days." It has been nine years since Ram's father left them for work never to return.

The boy slept for most parts of the first three days. He woke in between to eat and then slept again. Eventually on the third day, a Sunday, the boy woke up. Ram had the whole of the day planned. Their bonding, comfortingly, was instant.

As they ran out to play, Seema asked the boy his name and where he was from.

"Rahim is my name. The footpath is my home."

Over time, Ram and Rahim became inseparable. Their camaraderie was remarkable. In cricket, when at the crease together, they massacred the rival team. In school, they were among the smart ones.

One day in December of 1992, they played the parts of Ram and Rahim in their school stage performance. Ram became Rahim and Rahim was dressed as Ram. Their teacher was confused between their real and stage names, but the boys giggled: "Ma'am, both are the same. Ram is Rahim. Rahim is Ram."

After the performance, both boys still in their stage costumes, rushed to the field to play cricket—their favourite sport. The elders told the boys that it was not the best day to play cricket. Somewhere far away, a mosque was being razed to the ground. It was not safe to be out playing. But the boys, as boys their age are, persisted and played.

The elders were right. A crowd was gathering close to the field's boundary. Slogans about '*janmbhoomi*' filled the air. At some point the crowd turned into a mob. Ram and Rahim noticed the mob closing in on to them. Amidst them divided into two along community lines, the irony of their names stood out.

Surrounded from all sides, the boys were helpless, scared and confused. Ram was the first to speak to the mob: "Don't touch Rahim!" Rahim added: "And you dare not touch Ram!"

Oblivious of the land where an era was brought tragically to an end, Ram and Rahim stood like rocks, balanced in thought and action to protect each other till the end of life. As they took blows, the brothers defended each other like they had always done from times immemorial.

Historical Note: *On 6 December 1992, a large crowd of activists demolished the 16th-century Babri Mosque in the city of Ayodhya, leading to riots in India.*

Curiosity is
the wick in the candle of learning.
William Arthur Ward

uriosity

/kjʊərɪˈɒsɪti/ an eager wish to know or learn about something

A B **C** D E F G H I J K L M N O P Q R S T U V W X Y Z

CURIOSITY

Aaro loved his small garden. It was the best thing he liked in his new home. Even though it was small and rickety, he spent hours there.

The most curious object in his garden was the wild weed. Aaro's mother had told him to stay clear of that and never ever to touch the black wild fruit that grew on the weed. She said, "Fruits can change mankind like one did in the Garden of Eden!" She believed and therefore she warned Aaro that unusual and mysterious creatures lived below that wild weed. "Safety first, curiosity later... don't ever forget!"

His mother's directives made Aaro all the more curious. He would wonder day and night about the world that existed below that shrub. The more he thought, the more curious he got. An incessant cycle of thoughts and curiosity fuelled little Aaro's imagination.

One day, bound by his vow to his mother not to venture close to the weed, Aaro decided to explore the world below the weed in a different way. He started putting his imagination into a drawing. He drew what he could imagine of the dark unusual nether land below the wild shrub. His curiosity pushed his spirits, his dreams, his explorations, and gradually Aaro started to see amazing things beyond the realm of what his mother deemed appropriate. The more he drew, deeper he delved. The more he imagined, the more curious he got. Aaro was free-falling in the vortex of his curiosity and imagination.

It took him many days to finally complete the drawing. Aaro was happy. He went to his mother and showed her his new world—a world where mysterious men lived in harmony with each other, nature and animals of another kind.

Aaro's mother was mesmerised by what she saw. She took some time to comprehend the details of her son's imagination, which was unusual and different yet delightfully beautiful. "Son! Your curiosity is the wick of my learning. Go explore this beautiful world!" She allowed Aaro to venture beyond.

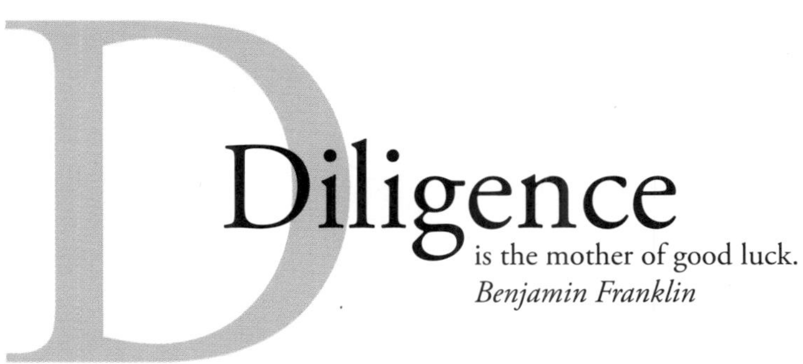

/ˈdɪlɪdʒ(ə)ns/ careful and persistent work or effort

A B C **D** E F G H I J K L M N O P Q R S T U V W X Y Z

DILIGENCE

Toral was a role model for Inaira. Everything Toral did, she did with perfection. Not only was she good in academics, but she also played tennis like a professional. In the pool, she swam like a fish and on the tracks, she was a breeze. Each of her drawings was worthy of a frame. That Inaira was in awe of Toral was evidently an understatement.

"Toral didi, how do you do everything so well?" Inaira asked one day. Toral smiled and avoided the adulation. "But you must tell me!" insisted Inaira. "It is very simple, my dear. Whenever an opportunity comes knocking, take it up diligently," Toral revealed her secret to the little one.

Inaira did not understand what it meant yet she rejoiced. She now had the mantra. The secret of Toral was now her's too. She danced in delight, rapt in thought that she was now empowered with her didi's secret, of being the best at everything.

The next day, Toral left for her home. But her secret resonated in Inaira's mind ever since. Inaira scribbled the secret on a chart and hung it on the wall facing her bed. "*Be Diligent!*" it read.

Years went by. The belief of childhood became even more pronounced in her teens. To the impressionable Inaira, Toral was the leitmotif of perfection and success. In her mind, Toral was the high benchmark of achievement and anything Inaira did never seemingly matched up to those exacting standards. Inaira started believing that probably she was not spotting the right opportunities.

More years went by. Almost a decade later, they met again at a family wedding. Inaira was now in her late teens while Toral had become a successful professional, working with a new-age technology company. They met and bonded immediately. At first, they smiled reservedly, which gradually gave way to hearty laughter when they reminisced about the days of childhood. Neither of them had forgotten any part of those days.

Once the ice was broken, Inaira could wait no more, and abruptly popped the ever baffling question: “But didi, you never told me when I would know if an opportunity was around. I could get diligent immediately on knowing that.”

Toral looked at Inaira and smiled as she did years ago. A decade had elapsed but both remembered that day when the secret was passed from one generation to the next. Toral smiled and said: “Diligence never waits for opportunity. It creates opportunity.” While Inaira was processing the words of wisdom, Toral didi added: “Be diligent *always*. Opportunity, I assure you, will never miss you then.”

Inaira beamed. The decoding of ‘the secret’ was finally complete.

E
Empathy
Empathy is about finding echoes of another person in yourself.
Mohsin Hamid
/ˈɛmpəθi/ the ability to understand and share the feelings of another
A B C D **E** F G H I J K L M N O P Q R S T U V W X Y Z

EMPATHY

Rooh and Rabba were the best of friends. Probably because their mothers were best friends too. Incidentally, Rooh and Rabba, like their mothers, were born in the same month, two weeks apart, of the same year. Rooh would delay her birthday celebration by a week and Rabba would advance hers by one to have a common date of celebration. Their eighth birthday was two months away.

This year was not the usual year. Rabba's mother had not been keeping well for the past many months. The doctors tried the best medicines, while members of the family took to prayers; but certain ailments heed neither. Rabba's mother was crumbling, and though death came, it took its time. She lost weight, her hair fell, her back stooped and one day she was bedridden. A month before Rooh and Rabba's common birthday that year, the remains of what used to be Rabba's beautiful and kind mother were buried.

It is difficult to say who of the two, Rooh or Rabba, cried more ever since. It was Rabba's loss but Rooh felt the pain alike. She was Rabba's mother but Rooh missed her dearly too. In the park where they played, the swings were not in tandem anymore. While Rabba stopped talking, Rooh sulked endlessly. Nothing and no one could soothe either of the girls.

On their birthday, Rooh always met Rabba first in the morning. This was Rooh's birthday ritual for as long as she could remember. She would go to Rabba's house along with her mother with a gift for her. Rooh carried the gift knowing that Rabba would have one ready for her too.

This year was different. Neither of them had any gift for the other. Yet they did meet like they always did. They sat quietly for a few minutes before Rooh's mother broke the silence and tried to brighten up the atmosphere.

After a few uncomfortable minutes of loud silence and muted conversation, it was time to leave. Rooh embraced Rabba and whispered in her ear, “I do have a gift for you but I could not pack it.” She held Rabba’s hand and put it into her mother’s, “I have got a mother for you this year.”

Rabba embraced Rooh and smiled. A smile which had sprung up after a long while, probably the first since her mother had died.

Rooh couldn’t have asked for a better gift in return.

This year too, like always, the friends had a gift for each other.

Freedom

is the oxygen of the soul.

Moshe Dayan

/ˈfriːdəm/ the condition or right of being able or allowed to do, say, think, etc. whatever you want to, without being controlled or limited

A B C D E **F** G H I J K L M N O P Q R S T U V W X Y Z

FREEDOM

Freedom is an elusive concept. Not for Eklavya though.

Having spent his life chained to his wheelchair, his freedom lay in being able, and if possible, to stand on his feet. Literally. Born without legs knee downwards, Eklavya saw the world around him walk, sprint, hurry, scurry, scuttle... but all he felt as he saw this world, was a tingly sensation at the stub that qualified as his knees.

This was the reason that today was a big day. Eklavya was as much delighted as he was afraid. He was a mixed bag of emotions. A voice inside his head said, "Why leave the safety and comfort of the chair!".

The other voice, straight from his heart, offered words of encouragement, "Run, Eklavya Run!"

"Don't you like being looked after?", the mind reasoned.

"Be independent, Eklavya!" cheered the heart.

Eklavya's courage finally prevailed over diffidence. He had the prosthetics fitted.

He shifted a bit in the new contraption, struggled a little and finally tried to stand, aided by the medical staff around him and the walker placed right in front of the wheelchair. The muscles in his neck and shoulders stiffened, his arms bulged and the heart thumped fast as he rose from the wheelchair and pushed his weight on to the walker. His body responded less from the physical exhaustion of trying to stand but more from the anticipation of what would happen next.

Gradually beads of sweat started forming on his forehead and the breadth became shallower. The strain colluded with the voice in the head and dictated, "Enough boy! Sit down! Now!"

The medical staff knew from experience that it is not easy to take the weight of the whole body on to the legs immediately. Besides, it required days to get used to standing on two legs. Therefore, they inched closer to Eklavya in order to help him sit down. It was enough for a day's work.

At the very moment, Eklavya released the grip on the walker and pushed it away gently. He took the weight of his body on his legs. He raised his chin and took a deep breath. The slight upward curve on either edges of his lip was raison d'être.

Freedom, an elusive concept but not for Eklavya, was being able to stand on his feet.

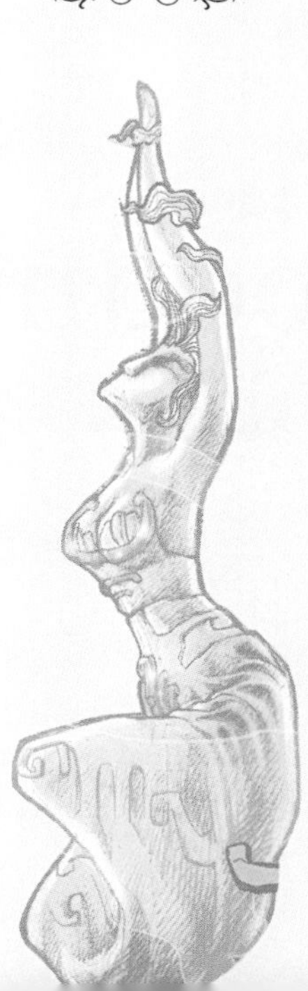

Goodness

does not flash, it glows.

Ray Stannard Baker

/ˈɡʊdnəs/ the personal quality of being morally good

A B C D E F **G** H I J K L M N O P Q R S T U V W X Y Z

WHEN HE SAW RAJU, THE EAGLET, TANGLED UP IN WIRE
HE KNEW IT WAS TIME FOR ANOTHER DOSE OF GOODNESS
HE FILLED HIMSELF TILL A GLOW SPREAD THROUGH HIM
HE USED THE ENERGY TO REACH DR. BAKSHI AT THE SPEED OF LIGHT
...THE END

GOODNESS

Nitin looked at his son Aakrit critically and said: "This plan is good but you have to be the best professional to save the bird."

He was referring to the eaglet that was caught in the barbed wire on their terrace.

Aakrit thought for a while before replying. "Papa, best is relative but good is absolute!", he said and headed to save the bird.

Nitin wanted to reply but could not find the right words. Besides, he was getting late for work. It was the month-end and the day would be a long one. With Diwali around, he had to clock the right numbers to be eligible for the big annual bonus. The three best employees at the firm would get the lion's share of the jackpot, while the rest would get little. To be the star in the sales division, Nitin had to soak in the month-end pressure every four weeks.

Nitin was consistent at his job, but his peer group was competitive. No one was certain who would finally make it to the top three this year. The company used a complex process. The final rankings on the leader-board involved discretionary inputs as well. Nitin did not fall in the category of people who would apple-polish their bosses. He was better at client interfacing than managing his superior. If he had an opinion, he voiced it. Nitin was not a 'Yes man'.

As he sat down with his boss, Nitin was dejected to hear that he did not make it to the final three. He had tried hard this time. He had promised Aakrit a motorbike and his wife a vacation in the Maldives. A big bonus would have helped pay for both.

Nitin's boss sensed his dejection. "You make me proud Nitin. There will be another year which will be yours. You are good but this year someone else is the best."

At that moment, Aakrit's eaglet flashed across Nitin's mind. He remembered that although Aakrit was committed to saving injured animals, he, as a father, always undermined his son's efforts, quite like his boss who undermined his contribution. Nitin managed to reply before leaving the supervisor's room: "Sir, *best* is relative but *good* is absolute."

Next day, the list of outperformers was declared. It had four names instead of the customary three.

No legacy is so rich as

honesty.

William Shakespeare

H

/ˈɒnɪsti/ the quality of being truthful, sincere and free of deceit

A B C D E F G **H** I J K L M N O P Q R S T U V W X Y Z

HONESTY

Growing up in a village as the only child of his parents, Bapi found friends in things inanimate. Loitering on the banks of the meandering river, walking through the thick woods and climbing obtuse trees took most of his time. He did have a few friends but being the zamindar's son, most of them kept a reserved distance from him. Consequently, Bapi was a lonesome child with a childhood bereft of playing in the mud or stealing mangoes from the neighbour's tree.

He had a few secret friends though—the trees around his house. Bapi knew the names of all of them. He had even coined pet names for each. The banyan tree, his favourite, in the botanical garden across the block was his 'best friend'.

On his twelfth birthday, he demanded from his father a 'new friend'—his very own banyan tree. His father tried to persuade him to ask for anything else. "A banyan tree will spread its roots deep and ruin our house in no time!" he reasoned with him. But Bapi, being an only child used to having his way, was unrelenting. He refused to acknowledge any argument, sweet talk or reprimand.

Finally, his parents relented. A banyan sapling soon arrived at the bungalow. It was planted in a large pot and placed in Bapi's room. Bapi tended to the sapling as a mother would to her newborn. The banyan plant reciprocated the attention it got and grew rapidly. In a few months' time, the new friend was ready to move into the spacious and sprawling front garden. Bapi carefully chose the spot where the tree was to be planted. Unfortunately, it was right in front of the main entrance of the bungalow—much to the distress of his parents who shuddered at the thought that in no time, the tree would cover the entrance and its roots would crack the walls of their centuries-old ancestral house. But they were powerless against their persistent child.

Years went by and the banyan tree grew and grew. The tree became the monstrosity that the zamindar had feared. However, little Bapi, now sixteen, loved it. When he was leaving for further schooling in England, like his father and grandfather had done before him, he hugged the banyan tree and watered its roots lovingly—

mostly with his tears. The zamindar and his wife felt a bit betrayed on not having received similar affection.

Years rolled by and the tree started blocking the entry to the bungalow. Initially, there were a few protests but gradually everyone got used to the inconvenience. Bapi would regularly enquire about his friend in his letters from England. With time, the enquiries waned much like the frequency of his letters.

Nevertheless, the banyan tree continued growing. The main entrance was now entirely blocked. The back entrance of the bungalow became the new approach to the house. The garden was untended and the once resplendent bungalow developed cracks.

After eight years, Bapi, now 24 years old, was returning home from England. He was no more a kid but the '*chotto zamindar*' (little landlord). The word had gone around in the village that their *chotto zamindar* was returning home with a '*gori memsahib*'. On the day of their arrival, the zamindar's wife looked at the banyan tree and wondered how a little plant had become a gigantic tree! Its roots had spread into the ancestral house and had cracked open the walls in many places. The zamindar could have cut the tree down but he did not have the heart to do so. In its growth, they saw Bapi growing. In its development, they saw Bapi prosper.

As the car approached the dilapidated bungalow, it detoured to the back entrance. The main entrance was no more accessible. Forced to take the back entrance to his own house, Bapi felt a bit ashamed... more so since he used to boast to his friends in England, "In my palatial house, the back door is for the servants."

When he reached the main foyer, he saw how the tree had spread into the walls of the house cracking it in places and creating a wreck of what was a splendid palace. At lunch that day, there was an uncomfortable silence at the table. Bapi finally spoke, "Baba, you must consider having the banyan tree cut down. To be honest, the tree is a parasite." He made eye contact sheepishly and continued, "Only a spoilt brat could have planted it in our beautiful garden. There is thankfully none in our family now."

The zamindar and his wife paused. They looked at each other in silence. The irony of their son's honesty left them speechless.

KRITI
integrity
is doing the
right thing even
when no one
is watch-
ing

Integrity

is doing the right thing,
even when no one is watching.
C. S. Lewis

I

/ɪnˈtɛgrɪti/ the quality of having strong moral principles

A B C D E F G H **I** J K L M N O P Q R S T U V W X Y Z

INTEGRITY

It was lunchtime and the lane near my office, popularly known as the 'food lane', was swarming with people. The lane catered to office workers like me whose search for a decent lunch at a reasonable price often led them to converge at the scores of food kiosks operating here. The lunchtime flurry in the lane lasted usually for an hour between 1 and 2 p.m. After 2 p.m., both the stall operators and their patrons disappeared, the former into the recesses of the metropolis from where they had emerged and the latter back to their work cubicles. This routine was repeated day in and day out throughout the work week.

Amidst the cacophonous chaos that prevailed in the lane during lunch time, one could barely notice an old lady. She stood at the end of the lane waiting expectantly with homemade offerings filled in two large multi-tiered tiffin boxes. Her bent spine and measured steps indicated a life of hardship and struggle. As I found out later, her day began with a walk of a few miles weighed down with heavy boxes. She would then take the crowded village train and an overflowing city bus to ultimately make a livelihood at the food lane.

When I noticed her for the first time, it was out of sheer pity. I felt sorry for her. Very few people came to her modest booth. One day, when I was in the mood to experience a different cuisine, I went to her stall and asked for a meal. She seemed pleased to have found a new patron. Soon enough, a piping hot thali was in front of me. It had everything that makes a meal complete and sumptuous. The food was simple yet very satisfying.

As I lit an after-meal cigarette, I began chatting with the old lady. "Why do you work so hard when you should be resting at your age?" I asked her. "I have outlived everyone in my life, beta," she answered, her crinkled face breaking into a toothless smile. She was ninety three years old. Her children, six of them, had all died—some succumbed to diseases and some to age. Her friends were also either six feet under or strewn across as ash. She had to work, she had no other choice, she had to make ends meet.

The more I frequented her stall, the more I liked the old lady. I started calling her '*Budima*' (Old Mother). Over time, I convinced a few of my colleagues to visit her as well.

One day when I approached her stall, she wasn't there. While I was wondering what must have happened, she came huffing, completely out of breath carrying her tiffin boxes. She was overtly apologetic about the delay and revealed almost in tears that she could not prepare '*paayas*' (a sweet dish made from milk and rice) that day. "I could not buy milk which is the main ingredient for preparing *paayas*," she told me over and over again as she laid out the thali. The absence of *paayas* did not bother me but her constant apology made me uncomfortable. I had my meal hurriedly, paid her and was about to leave when she stopped me and held out her feeble hand with some change in it.

"What is this?" I asked in surprise.

"Your balance money, beta. Because I could not make *paayas* for you, I cannot take the full amount of the meal."

"I can't accept this," I said, refusing to take back the small change.

"Please take this money, beta. I will not be comfortable unless you do. I have lived a life full of hardships but one of principles. I did not serve you a complete meal today. So how can I accept full money for the meal?" she reasoned, forcing the money into my hands.

I stood there looking at her weather-beaten face. It had assumed a soft glow that I presume comes from having led a life of uncompromising integrity.

If you carry

joy

in your heart,
you can heal any moment.

Carlos Santana

/dʒɔɪ/ great happiness

A B C D E F G H I **J** K L M N O P Q R S T U V W X Y Z

JOY

Sahar's mother held a mirror and asked "Sahar, what do you see? How do you feel?"

Sahar looked at herself in the mirror and giggled. "It's perfect," she exclaimed. Her new phiran looked beautiful and the scarf complimented it perfectly. It was a special day—Sahar had turned sixteen. She had carefully chosen the phiran—a gift from her Baba and Amma. It had a rich orange colour much like the shade of the saffron flowers growing in the field behind her house. An intricate layout of floral embroidery on the neck and sleeves accentuated its look.

"I can't wait for my friends to see me", gushed Sahar as she ran through the lanes as happy as a clam at high water. She was an effusive bundle of joy. It was as if waves of energy flowed through her and charged all those who came in touch with her. That day, she was the beautiful lass of Kashmir.

The lane from Sahar's house opened onto the main road. There was a huge crowd at the square, but in her exuberance, Sahar barely noticed it. She simply flowed with the milieu towards her school. She sang with joy, oblivious to the throngs of people surrounding her, "O Sahar, what's your journey? O Sahar, where will life take you?"

Thak! Thak! The shots suddenly rang out. They were pellets meant to disperse protesters. The crowd was not celebratory as Sahar had imagined, it was a gathering of protesters.

Thak! Thak! Sahar felt a piercing pain as a pellet hit her eye and she dropped down unconscious.

Dhak! Dhak! When she opened her eyes, she could hear her heartbeat. Then she heard Baba and Amma. But she could not see them. She saw only darkness. The pellets had done more than what they were supposed to do. Sahar was devastated. She was not blind. She was blinded.

The doctors could not help her much but her treatment continued. The selfless support of Baba and Amma taught Sahar to live in darkness. She did not run anymore. Gradually, she learnt to smell the air, hear the sounds and feel the world. No more a bundle of joy, she was a symbol of everything that had gone wrong in the beautiful valley.

Five years had gone by since that fateful day. Sahar had forgotten the appearance of a lot of things. She forgot how Baba and Amma looked. She had even forgotten her own face. She had forgotten the redness of the rose and the green colour of the grapes. She had forgotten the white of the snow and the hue of the sunset. Sahar's birthday was no more a day to be celebrated. No matter how much she tried, the date reminded her of the tragedy.

"Will today be different?" Sahar wondered. A pair of eyes donated to her by a dying aunt could make her see again. Would her new eyes undo the pain of the past too?

The doctor said the operation had been successful. While the dressing was being removed, Baba and Amma held Sahar's hands. At first, she could only see the white. She tried to focus but saw nothing. Was whiteness her new darkness? Gradually the new eyes learnt to focus again and she saw a blurry figure. It was Baba, but how old he looked! Amma's worried face had many more wrinkles than she remembered. Yet Sahar was smiling as tears rolled from her eyes.

The nurse held a mirror and asked, "Sahar, what do you see? How do you feel?"

"Baba, I see hope! Amma, I feel joy." Sahar replied incoherently in-between sobs. She gushed with child-like exuberance like the good old days.

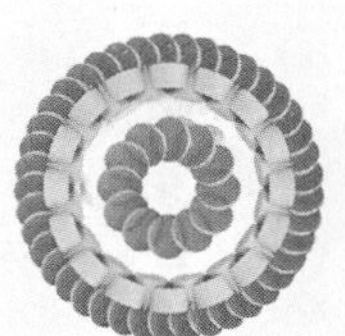

No act of
kindness,
no matter how small, is ever wasted.
Aesop

/ˈkʌɪn(d)nəs/ the quality of being friendly, generous, and considerate

A B C D E F G H I J **K** L M N O P Q R S T U V W X Y Z

KINDNESS

The Manhattan skyline is an inspiration for any artist. As one belonging to the fraternity, I feel peaceful every time I look down at the sprawling city from my high-rise bay window. I love this city yet I miss my home town Udaipur. In 1829, Colonel James Tod, the East India Company's first political agent in the region, had remarked Udaipur to be "the most romantic spot on the continent of India."* It indeed is! With several magnificent palaces and lakes, Udaipur has a rich heritage built by the kindness of its people. This story is about one such kind person—Bansuri Bhaiya (The Flute Player).

I grew up playing in the narrow, labyrinthine lanes of beautiful Udaipur. I cannot recall having a formal schooling until I was over 10 years old. I vividly remember the dusky evenings I spent plunging in the Pichola Lake with my friends. We would play there until our mothers came whining and dragged us out by our ears. In those joyous evenings, the air used to overflow with mesmerizing non-stop melody from the flute of the Bansuri Bhaiya.

There are different genres of music. The one that lingers in our minds the most, more often than not, has some memory attached to it. Bansuri Bhaiya's melody is the key to my memories of a joyous childhood spent with family and friends. Bansuri Bhaiya's music transcended time. It still reminds me of the happiness in the years gone by. Recollection of these memories brings a smile to me even in my dull days.

So strong is my attachment to The Flute Player's music that I feel compelled to go to Udaipur every year and listen to him live at dusk. It has been over three decades and I have not missed a year of this nostalgic journey. I have tried recording his melody to recreate the same world in Manhattan but in vain.

Last year when I saw him, he Flute Player had grown old and weak. Arthritis made his joints a burden. Initially the pain was manageable but over time it was difficult to bear. He could barely walk, yet he continued playing the melodies. He took to playing the flute while riding his motorbike. Now his son rode pillion, his drums in rhythm with the flute. Old age had also reduced the maestro's ability to

* *https://www.lonelyplanet.com/india/rajasthan/udaipur*

blow and retain air in the lungs. Consequently his tunes mellowed down. Over time, the melodies became incoherent. One day the music stopped. Forever.

I managed to find the Flute Player's small house in the thickly populated and dilapidated locality of the old city. I was welcomed in by his son. Between sips of tea and niceties I asked him, "What was it that motivated your father to play the flute so selflessly?" He said, "In his youth when Baba used to play the flute for the Maharana of Udaipur, the Maharana had ordained Baba to spread kindness in the city till Baba's last breath. The Maharana had assured him that so long as he spread kindness he could live in his kingdom peacefully." The son paused, looked at the flute and continued, "Baba always liked playing the flute but that day onwards, he was on a mission... a mission to spread kindness. I think this became his calling. Perhaps that was what really motivated him." He looked at me expectantly and asked, "Sir, do you believe my father achieved his mission?"

"Indeed. He did." I agreed in awe.

To
love
oneself is the beginning of a lifelong romance.
Oscar Wilde

/lʌv/ a great interest and pleasure in something or somebody

A B C D E F G H I J K **L** M N O P Q R S T U V W X Y Z

LOVE

Radha's birth coincided with a crucial blow to her life—the death of her mother.

Therefore, Aditya, her father, took time to love Radha. But when he did, he loved her more than anybody else. Perhaps even more than he had loved her mother.

As a sales agent in a small detergent company, Aditya could barely make ends meet. He wondered, at times, if his wife died because he could not provide well for her. Radha's mother was intrinsically frail and pregnancy made her weak. She had to do odd jobs during her pregnancy, since Aditya's earnings could not provide for the added medical expenses. Somewhere, deep in her heart, she knew that the price of having Radha would be her own life.

As a single parent, life was tough for Aditya. Yet he left no stone unturned to keep Radha close to his heart. He had lost his love once. He did not want to lose it again. Being motherless was tough for Radha too. She grew up in crèches and in the silence of their small house. Her father was out the whole day at work. By the time he returned, Radha would be asleep. Aditya knew that Radha was missing out on her childhood but the harsh truth of his life rendered him helpless. He would come home exhausted, open the door silently, and see Radha asleep always. Some days he would cry silently. He would stroke her head and try to sing lullabies as her mother would have done. Sometimes Radha would hold her father's hand gently while she heard the lullabies deep in her sleep. Aditya found redemption in these unconscious acts of affection.

Years passed. Life repeated its monotony. The day Radha graduated and got a coveted job in another country, Aditya was stoic, not knowing whether to be happy or sad. Radha had to leave in a few days. She had grown wings and was ready to discover a life beyond her father.

Radha did well at her job. In time she fell in love and married an American colleague. Over the next few years, Radha had her own family complete with three children. She would call Aditya regularly and they would have their usual talks, mostly in monosyllables. There was much to say but theirs was a relationship of unspoken understanding. A life spent struggling and surviving sapped out the niceties of healthy long conversations. Once Radha offered to send tickets to her father but Aditya declined to visit. He was too timid to venture beyond the confines of the known neighbourhood. He continued living in his single room apartment trapped in his memories.

Radha married an American, a colleague in her office who she fell in love with. She had sent tickets for her father but Aditya was too timid to venture beyond the confines of the neighbourhood. Over years, Radha had her own family complete with three children. Her father continued living in his small one room house back home trapped in his memories.

One day, Radha received a call that her father had a stroke and may not survive. In that moment her whole childhood flashed by. She remembered how her father would come home tired, yet celebrate the time with her. She took the first flight home and prayed all the way. When the plane landed, she rushed to the hospital. She had mostly seen her father helpless but that day he was even more so. The doctor briefed Radha of the reality and politely asked her if they should pull the plug as her father's chances of survival were next to nil. Tears welled up in her eyes. Radha did not know how to respond. She went near her father and stroked his head. Instinctively she hummed a song—the same lullabies that her father used to sing to her. She had slept through the lullabies in her childhood but she remembered the words and the tune to this day. She went back in time to her lonely past. Only, this time, the roles had reversed. The doctors and nurses left the room. Radha continued to hum through the night.

Next morning the beeps from the ward were much lesser and the green indicators outnumbered the red. All parameters on the screen were bordering on normal. The doctor on duty told Radha: "Surprisingly, even today when everything else fails, love cures miraculously."

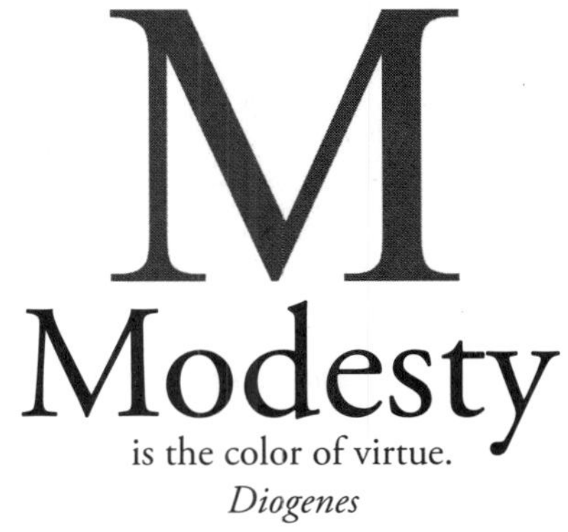

Modesty

is the color of virtue.

Diogenes

ˈmɒdɪsti/ behaviour, manner, or appearance intended to avoid impropriety or indecency

A B C D E F G H I J K L **M** N O P Q R S T U V W X Y Z

MODESTY

Jamal was a fisherman's son. He had grown up playing by the sea. His day would start in the wee hours. With his father on their small dinghy, he would help cast the net in the hope of a bountiful catch.

The sea was abundantly rich with crabs. "Catching crabs is not easy," Jamal's father would say while holding up his left hand with three fingers missing. He would narrate stories of his combat with the crabs and how their claws claimed his fingers - one each decade over the past thirty years. Jamal grew up hearing these stories. He had become a champion crab-catcher. Jamal had learnt everything they could do. He made no fuss about his skill and brushed away praises with a smile. He was modest both in speech and in mannerism.

In his youth, almost 40 years ago, Jamal was enterprising and ambitious. He wanted to own a large trawler. He took a sizeable loan from the village moneylender and got a trawler. In it, he would catch, clean and pack crabs to be exported far and wide. He employed several fishermen and took good care of them. They hailed him as their messiah. But he never saw anything extraordinary in his enterprise. Modesty, as before, was his shield.

Not everyone was happy with Jamal's progress. One stormy night, around 30 years back, his trawler broke the ropes and drifted to the rocky end of the beach. It breached into the sharp blades of the rocks and sank. The rumour was that the cunning moneylender and the jealous rivals had colluded to sink Jamal's trawler. Jamal, however, maintained that it was God's will. He had to sell his ancestral land to pay off part of the debt. He also started working on a boat to pay off the rest of the debt. Jamal worked hard day and night without any ill-will or vengeful thought. Modesty was ingrained in him.

With no land, spiralling debt and hard work, Jamal suffered a harsh life of humiliation. He was disillusioned by the drastic turn of destiny. One night, couple of decades ago, his father - poor, unhappy and unable to bear hardships in old age - died. His father's death broke his spirit. He took to meditation. Initially, he meditated to soothe his nerves. With time, he meditated to forget the past.

Gradually, he took to deep meditation as an effective tool to deal with his pain.

Jamal became distant at work. He gradually lost interest in his job, therefore quit it and became a hermit. Now penniless, he chose to move to a remote natural cave near the turbulent part of the sea. The cave became home for him. Always found meditating, Jamal became the village recluse, erased from the memories of the his folks. Over time, the villagers called him the recluse saint and only sympathized with what he had been through. Jamal never uttered a word. He accepted everything as God's will.

All the good work that Jamal, now close to fifty years of age, had done for his community was gradually forgotten. Sometimes the elderly would talk of old times, but they were considered senile anyway. "Once a recluse, always a recluse" went the local saying. And that was how the new breed identified Jamal– 'A Recluse'.

One day, while sneaking close to the abode of the 'Recluse', a child slipped and fell into the turbulent sea. The same sea that teemed with crabs. News of the accident spread like wild fire. The village women shouted for help, but none could muster the courage to get into the sea to save the child in peril.

Jamal heard the cries for help coming from the sea. He had grown in these waters. The sea was his playground. He dived in with a thought and rode the waves as Poseidon would have. He engaged with the crabs like a seasoned warrior to bring the child ashore—alive and unharmed.

But Jamal was bleeding and had deep cuts all over his body. Like his father, he had lost three fingers in the battle. The villagers were stunned. They stood undecided, not knowing how to react to the Recluse's act of bravery. Then, one old lady came forward and started bandaging his bleeding fingers with a piece of cloth. Someone among them hailed Jamal and gradually the whole village joined in the hurray.

No more accustomed to adulation, and with no one to talk to for years, Jamal took time to gather words and mumbled, "Any of you would do the same. I happened to be closest to the accident site." He tried to smile at the new found acceptance from his community.

To this day, in the main square of the village, you will find the statue of a smiling fisherman resembling Jamal, proudly holding a crab in his hand. The plaque reads: "Modesty is the colour of virtue. ~ Diogenes."

N

Naivety

is the first truth of aesthetics.

Friedrich Nietzsche

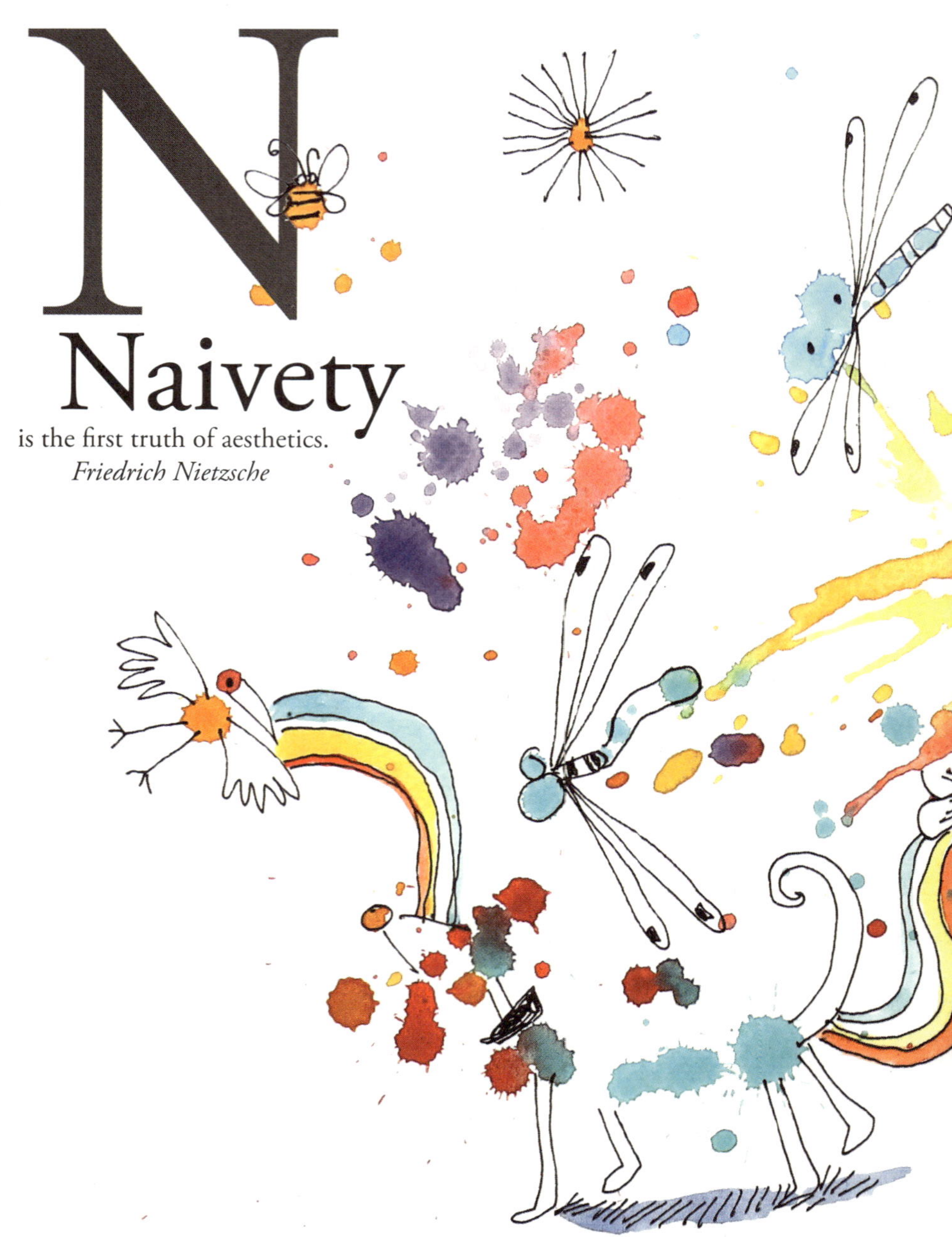

/nʌɪˈiːvti/ trust or action based on not having much experience

A B C D E F G H I J K L M **N** O P Q R S T U V W X Y Z

NAIVETY

Kiann's mother was an artist. A renowned one. Trained at a leading art school, her style had evolved over the years and it was unique. Her paintings brought her fame as well as money.

His father was an author, though not as famous. Self-taught in the school of life, his writing was an inspired mix of the styles of stalwarts before him. Unfortunately, his work barely got noticed.

Kiann's mother hoped to pass on her skills to her son. But Kiann was a wild one. He abhorred the discipline that was required of an artist. He had grown accustomed to seeing his mother concealed by the easel and his father buried behind piles of books. He preferred being out in the open, not hidden by easels and books.

His mother was persistent and that annoyed him. One day when she was trying to make Kiann practice art structurally, he told her to her face, "I am not you... I don't enjoy painting as you do." She ignored the outcry, deeming it childish. After all, what else would an eleven year old know! She tried to coax him, "Draw something. Just draw anything you wish to."

Kiann threw a fit. How could his mother be so obtuse! He ran to protest to his father. Engrossed in his readings, his father always had a solution, inspired like his work, from his readings. He told Kiann, "You can draw, if you try. Preserve your naivety, though. Let your innocence show."

Exasperated and more confused than before, Kiann stomped through the main hall and locked himself in his room. He soaked his brush and splashed colours all around, some on the canvas and more on the walls of the room. His mother raised an eyebrow in despair. His father wished him goodnight and murmured some more unsolicited wisdom incoherently.

Disappointed by the outcome of the day, Kiann sat looking at the splatter of colours strewn all over. He gradually fell into a deep slumber. In his dream,

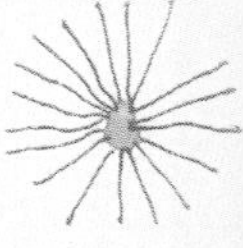

he was chasing dragonflies in a valley filled with bright flowers. The sun was dazzling that wintry morning and Whoffy, his timid pet mongrel, jumped around excitedly. The bees buzzed and the birds chirped, as dandelions floated in the crisp cool air.

Kiann woke up serene in the early hours of the next morning. Fresh out of his dream and well-rested, he was calm. He saw things clearly now. He drew outlines around the splatter of colours strewn on the canvas. A reflection of his dream—with bees, birds and flowers—took shape. A colourful story came alive. A beautiful art was ready.

Kiann pondered for a suitable name for his first art. "Naivety!" he exclaimed happily.

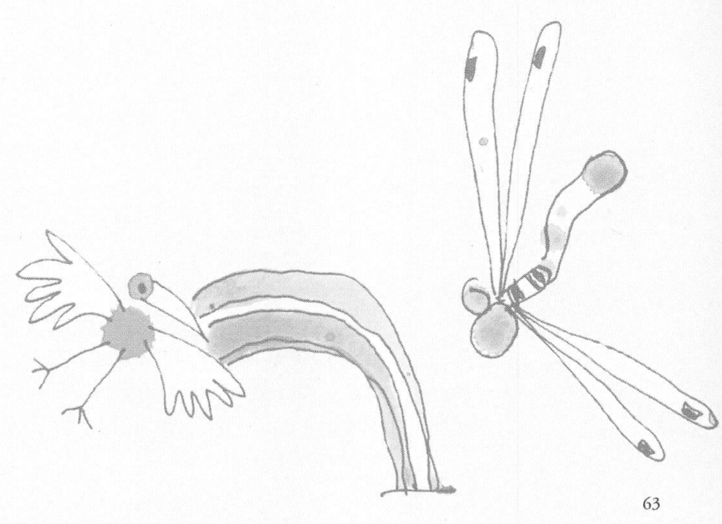

The earth is my altar,
The sky is my dome,
Mind is my garden,
The heart is my home
And I'm always at home…
Yea, I'm always at

Eden Ahbez

/əʊm/ a mystic syllable,
considered the most sacred mantra in Hinduism and Buddhism

A B C D E F G H I J K L M N **O** P Q R S T U V W X Y Z

OM SHANTI

It had been a painful pregnancy with the twin foetuses kicking hard and endlessly. Radha and Veer were understandably relieved when their boys Rajveer and Raghuveer were finally born. But they failed to see the signs, and were probably not familiar with the proverb—"Coming events cast their shadows before."

The fight that had begun in the womb continued. The boys fought with each other constantly and everywhere—at play, in the school, in the temple, at the market, you name it! If one cried, the other smiled at his brother's discomfort. When one rejoiced, the other sulked. The next fight, never too far away, was easily begun and fought with even more vigour. No amount of love or reprimand from either Radha or Veer made the children bicker less.

The frequency of fights increased as the boys grew. Veer was summoned to the headmaster's room often. He would see his sons on their knees outside the headmaster's room, shirts untucked and hair ruffled. By the time the boys reached their teens, Veer and Radha had accepted their ineptitude in restoring peace between the twins.

Eventually the parents decided to keep the boys apart in the hope that distance would achieve what extensive counselling could not. They decided that Rajveer would accompany his father to work in the field and Raghuveer would help his mother make earthen pottery at home. Peace prevailed so long as the brothers were kept away from each other.

They entered adulthood, developing their own skills, with Rajveer becoming a matchless tiller and Raghuveer excelling at pottery. One day, Radha died of old age and Veer followed her soon after. Unfortunately, this led to a graver situation!

That year the rains came early, the pottery would not dry and Raghuveer suffered. If the rains were late, the crops withered and Rajveer would be in distress. Hardship typically brings a family together, like hardships did for Radha and Veer, but the twin's case was complicated. The battle that had begun in the womb continued. Facing an imbalance of incomes almost every year, as per the whims of the rain God, the twins found reason to be miffed again and again.

One evening, a monk, on his way to the mountains, decided to spend the night in the village. It had been a scorching day—the rains were delayed by a couple of weeks. The monk rested under the tree outside Rajveer and Raghuveer's house. At dawn, he woke up with a start when he heard loud noises of the two brothers quarrelling. Curious, he strained his ears for details. He overheard Raghuveer mocking Rajveer about his current penurious state, while Rajveer reminded his twin about the previous year, when the rains had arrived early and Raghuveer had come pleading to him.

The monk was wise and he understood why the brothers fought ceaselessly. When nature brought them together, it ensured that they had to share everything. They shared the same womb, the same birth date, the same bed and the same upbringing. To be able to live with resources that always required sharing, however the twins had developed a strong primal instinct to survive, sadly, at the cost of each other's peace. The wise monk decided to help them.

Later that day, a monk landed at the twin's doorstep, asking for alms. He noticed the parapet that had divided the house into two sections. When the brothers came out to attend to him, the old monk said, "My lovely sons, I had known your kind and noble parents. They took care of me when I was in this village many years back." On hearing this, the twins invited the monk to their respective homes but, alas, they quarrelled again as to who would host the monk first.

The wise monk intervened immediately, "Om Shanti! Peace! Nature has turned you brothers against each other. Whether rains come early or late, one of you will suffer. You share resources among yourselves from the very beginning, and at times, the resources may be limited. My able children, know that Nature has ensured that you two always be together. Together you are twice as good, twice as wise and twice as strong. You are like yin and yang. Share your victories and failures alike and prosperity will be your ally. This is God's design."

The monk then turned and left for the mountains chanting, "Om Shanti! Peace!". The twins stood there considering the wise monk's counsel. For the first time in their lives, they found quaint reverberations of his chanting in their hearts. Later that day, they broke the parapet that divided them.

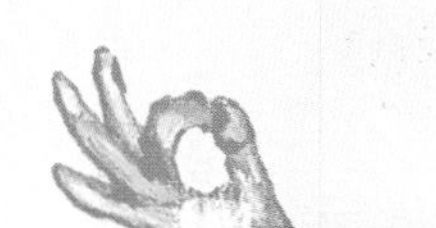

PER
SIST
ENC
E
Carry On Regardless.

Persistence

is to the character of man as
carbon is to steel.
Napoleon Hill

/pəˈsɪst(ə)ns/ the fact of continuing in an opinion or course of action in spite of difficulty or opposition

PERSISTENCE

The old bungalow was being razed. A skyscraper was going to come up there. The slum adjacent to the bungalow was to be razed next. The slum dwellers were safe for now.

The *raddiwala* from the slum was quick to grab the precious artefacts in the bungalow at throwaway prices. Among the steals was a grand piano. Too large for his tiny *kholi*, the piano seemed fated to be taken apart. In a rare moment of sanity, however, the *raddiwala* decided to keep the piano intact. He hoped of making a fortune someday by selling it as an antique masterpiece.

The *raddiwala* prepared a makeshift roof supported by bamboo poles to protect the grand piano from the weather. The covering would also protect the piano from the prying eyes of the slum dwellers. Small creepers placed at the base of the poles ensured that the canine residents of the neighbourhood did not mark their territories anywhere close.

However, all efforts to keep the piano inconspicuous were in vain. The beautiful piece commanded the attention of one and all. The slum dwellers had seen such a magnificent instrument only in the movies. To be able to feel the wood and ivory keys was a privilege for them.

Urban residents usually don't have space for a grand piano in their boxed beehives they call home. The ones who do have space don't have second-hand things in their lives. Over time, when the piano could not find a home, the *raddiwala* started to worry. The piano had become a liability, mocking his acumen right under his nose. People's interest in the piano also waned with time. Over time, the creepers around it grew to cover the piano like wild weed. The masterpiece now lay neglected and decrepit.

Jacob, a composer, had moved to the 'city of dreams' long ago as a young and enthusiastic lad. After years of struggle, Jacob's dreams faded a bit but he continued and persisted nevertheless. Destiny mocked him, fate ridiculed his efforts at composing and success refused to befriend him. At age seventy-eight, on the outside, Jacob seemed like another one, like many others, who had surrendered his dreams to the realities of survival. But on the inside, and in his mind, Jacob believed that his day would come.

That day, while he sipped tea at the corner stall, Jacob peeped at the piano and wished to run his rusty fingers over its keys. After some hesitation, he mustered the courage to break ice with the *raddiwala*. The sun had set and it was getting dark. The children were returning home from play, the women were cooking in their kitchens and the men were jostling back from work. Amidst the usual humdrum activities of what was 'just another day', suddenly a soothing melody filled the air. Initially the low notes flowed, followed by the middle ones and finally the maestro peaked and hit the ivory keys like a young and enthusiastic lad. Jacob played on for a while. His music permeated through every ear in the vicinity.

From that day onwards, Jacob was at the piano regularly. The *raddiwala* liked the attention his masterpiece received. A few people mocked old Jacob yet he persisted to play his original compositions interlaced with popular music of the times. No one escaped the charm of the trebles and the clefs. The children were Jacob's best audience. With gaping eyes, open mouths and curious minds, they giggled, cheered and clapped along when Jacob played.

The sound of music became a routine for the slum dwellers. Everyone wished to have a part of the melody in their lives. The clogged windows of the hutments opened up to let the music flow. People could now be seen through these open windows, relaxed in their chairs reunited with their forgotten dreams. Hope revived everywhere. Jacob's music was a balm which did more than just soothe... It healed. It made one and all believe again. It made everyone dream again.

The *raddiwala* eventually found value in his investment. Jacob too finally found a rapt audience. Their persistence had paid off.

/kwɛst/ a long or arduous search for something

A B C D E F G H I J K L M N O P **Q** R S T U V W X Y Z

Q

The greatest
quest
in life is to reach
one's potential.
Mychal Wynn

Brajesh rode the waves at sea. Much of his adult life passed in the engine room of a merchant ship. He would have been content sailing had he not have to stop at ports with pretty girls sashaying, curious youngsters giggling and spirited men cheering. In their happiness, he longed for his own. He brooded over how his youth was passing by all alone.

Mostly, he missed Manju, his childhood friend. Manju and Brajesh were neighbours first; in time, they became classmates; and later, friends. When they entered college, their relationship blossomed in between the daily routine—while sharing tiffin at school, or while exchanging notes in college. At times, Brajesh would leave a flower petal between the pages of the notebook he shared with Manju; she would reciprocate with half-erased love signs or romantic couplets in between the pages. Both of them knew but neither confessed.

On the day of their college graduation, Manju proposed to Brajesh. He smiled hesitantly but remained silent. He needed a firm professional footing before he could get into a binding relationship. He was also confused: what if there was someone else for him? His silence hardened Manju—something between them had changed. The chasm became deeper when Brajesh left for the sea.

One evening, the ship sailed out from another lively port, with Brajesh and his heavy heart. His ship made its way steadily into the vast ocean ahead and the port was now only a small speck in the far horizon. The sun had set; the dying rays painted the sky a melancholic hue. Brajesh decided to take a final round of the engine room before calling it a day. He whiled away his time checking gauges in the machinery space; his mind wandered to an imagined life he would have many years hence. He was lost in his daydream, the routine hum of the machines and the splashing sounds of the waves kept growing. "God, Give me a sign! What will my life be?"

It was at the lowermost platform of the machinery space where he noticed that the cap of the bilge tank sounding pipe was missing. A quick search ensued; the cap was rolling gently nearby. As he bent to pick it up, he accidentally nudged it further into a small opening to the dirty bilges below. "Arrgh!" he grunted. "What's the chance that a cap rolling for hours remains on the platform, but on being found, slips into the bilge! Such an amazing luck I have!"

He grudgingly lifted the heavy metal opening in the bottom platform to enter the ship's nether regions. Minutes passed but Brajesh's search yielded nothing. The heat below and the oily stench added to his frustration. He decided to climb back up onto the lower platform. As one final attempt, he flashed the torch again into the bilges. He flustered, "Damn! Give me a sign!"

Brajesh's torch flashed on to a gleaming surface where he could see the word 'LOST' written clearly. He looked hard to be sure that he had read it right. Was his God finally communicating with him? Was this the divine sign he had asked for? A fright gripped over Brajesh. He quickly ascended the stairs, a bit shaken, and as he passed the bilge tank sounding pipe in deep thought, he saw a new cap already in place on the sounding pipe! Alone in the machinery space, Brajesh was a lot shaken now.

He slept little, that starry night. The next morning, he asked the crew to find the missing cap. One of the men came back within minutes. "Sir, here it is. The cap was rolling near the Lube Oil Sump Tank (LOST) in the bilges. I had come for my night rounds yesterday and found the cap missing. So, I had put a new one there. What should I do with this old cap, Sir?"

Brajesh took the old cap in his hand and smiled. He realized that he had seen 'LOST' written on the manhole of the '**L**ube **O**il **S**ump **T**ank'. He had found what he was looking for. He hurried to the ship's radio room and called Manju. His heart was racing when the phone bell rang. Manju's "Hello!" calmed him a little. He hesitated and said, "Manju, I am ready."

Manju waited for what seemed to be a long pause. She gulped the lump in her throat and replied, "I will inform my parents." Content and at peace with each other, they held their phones tight, listening to the occasional sighs in the pervading silence—their feelings now uncaged, travelled the chasm of geographical separation between them; no words were needed—they thought.

Two lost souls, deeply in love ended their quest as they found each other again.

Knowledge will give you power, but character

respect.

Bruce Lee

/rɪˈspɛkt/ admiration felt or shown for someone or something that you believe has good ideas or qualities

A B C D E F G H I J K L M N O P Q **R** S T U V W X Y Z

रुमाल

कोई तपती धूप में
पोंछे पसीने को

कोई हाथ साफ़ करे
फिर से गंदा करने को

कोई नाक ख़ाली कर दे अपनी
तो कोई दे रोते को

कोई बाँध आँख पर अपने
ढूँढ़े सपनों को

कोई बाँध पोटली यादों की
ढूँढ़े अपनों को

छोटा ना समझ इस टुकड़े को
ख़ुद छोटा हो जाएगा

जितना देगा मान तू इसको
रूह माल समझ तू पाएगा

- अनुज शर्मा

Respect

Some in scorching heat
Use it to wipe off sweat

Others clean their hands
Yet to soil them again

Some use it to blow their nose
And others to wipe tears

While some blind their eyes with it
so they can dream

Others collect memorabilia in it
To remember memories lost

Think not of it as a small cloth
Because your thought makes you small

The more the respect you give
The more the soul you will find

-Anuj Sharma

RESPECT

Miss Khanna was known to select abstract topics for the elocution class. The topic that week was 'short yet tall'. Rather unusual, wasn't it? This was perhaps why Vikramaditya declared Miss Khanna to be the best teacher. Being predictably unpredictable was a trait that they shared.

Vikramaditya had a logistic disadvantage. Alphabetically, his turn came way down in the class roster. By the time his name would be called, the class would have heard just about everything that could be said about the topic. Only Zakir would be left to speak after Vikramaditya. And Zakir was the predictable kind. It did not matter to him if his words echoed what had already been narrated. But for Vikramaditya, repetition or any similarity to his words was by his own standards a humiliating letdown. Therefore, Vikramaditya would always be anxious till his turn came. All through the others' speeches, he would hope that no one would say anything close to the lines that he had prepared.

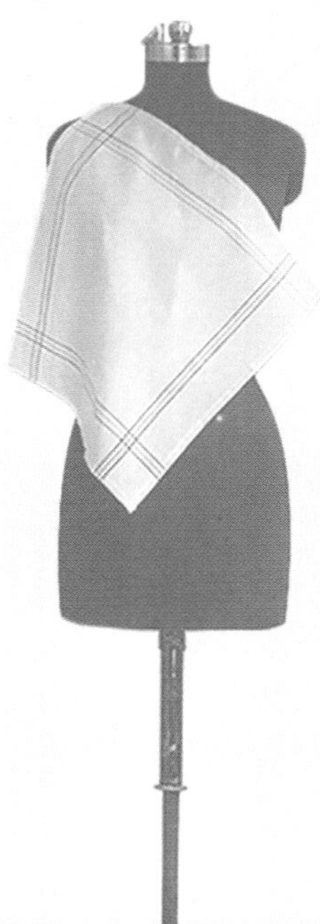

In the 'short yet tall' elocution class, multiple interesting perspectives were presented. Dolly talked about the cricket player who, though short in height, set tall records. Hridey talked about the cat whose tiny body rarely prevented it from jumping across tall structures. Jigar amazed everyone with the story of a mango tree, born of a small seed, which grew to be the tallest tree in the village. Pranit had a tale to narrate about his younger brother who, though vertically challenged, made tall claims of fame and feats. Many other fascinating tales kept the young minds humoured and engrossed.

When Vikramaditya's turn came, there was palpable silence in the class. His mates knew well that Vikramaditya would present a singular perspective. Miss Khanna too waited in anticipation to hear Vikramaditya's unusual point of view. Her amused smile revealed the expectation she had.

"I have a short one-line narration today and I hope its effect on us is anything but that." Vikramaditya waited for the words to sink in while he stood in front of the class.

"Respect—a short word—whether given or received, is a tall accomplishment," he said.

Sincerity

is the face of the soul.

Joseph Sanial-Dubay

sɪnˈsɛrəti/ the absence of pretence, deceit, or hypocrisy

A B C D E F G H I J K L M N O P Q R **S** T U V W X Y Z

SINCERITY

"Shanti, whatever you do, you must do it sincerely. It will take you places," assured father.

Eight-year-old Shanti heard intently but could not make much sense of what was said to her. Her earliest memory as a child was of clearing garbage at the skyscraper located close to the slum where she lived with her parents. She believed her job to be the best that could be.

Every morning, she tailed her father and mother in the wee hours to clear the bins flat by flat. In her parents, she saw idols who toiled to keep the neighbourhood clean. Some of the waste they collected could be exchanged for money which would buy them food for that day. Any windfall earning ensured a piece of sweet, which Shanti loved the most, but got only occasionally. Shanti wished to be like her father and mother when she grew older

She realized early in her life that she was not like the other children; she did not go to school. That bothered her at times, but not as much when the other children walked away from her as if she did not exist. She would draw their attention by waving at them yet no one acknowledged her presence. She had once overheard a boy say that being touched by her, or even by her shadow, could make one impure. The children often talked about a boy in their housing society who was once made to undergo '*shuddhi*', a ritual of purification, after Shanti had touched the ball he was playing with. Nevertheless, Shanti smiled and waved at them sincerely, without any ill feeling, in the hope that a day would come when she would be 'one among them'.

Shanti's life went on, overlooked by almost everyone around her. She would often wonder how her shadow—her constant companion, could vilify anyone? Could she ever get rid of her touch or shadow? While playing with a skipping rope one day, Shanti would see her shadow leave her for a moment, till she landed and connected again with it. She wondered if she would ever be able to leave the impure shadow behind.

One rainy season, plague engulfed the slums. Those were the days of total lockdown—no slum dweller was allowed anywhere around the buildings. The apartheid was even more rigid within the slum. People shunned the likes of Shanti as untouchables. Within a span of two weeks, Shanti's parents succumbed to high fever. A few old women branded Shanti as the evil one who had consumed her own parents, and sent her away to an orphanage.

Here, she met many other children like herself—mostly ragpickers and garbage collectors. They all had two things in common—the irony of her fate and a life bereft of a happy childhood.

A few months went by when, an Australian couple visited the orphanage. They talked politely and with respect. They even bought new clothes and toys for the children. Shanti was very happy but confused. All her life, she had only picked used clothes and broken toys from the bins and mended those for her use. Just when she had learnt to remain stoic and accept life as it came, this had happened. It made her wonder why anyone would be so generous.

The next day, Shanti learnt that the couple she had met were keen to adopt her—they would be leaving soon after the mandatory paperwork was done. Though Shanti had found herself a family—a place to call home, she had doubts whether she would ever become 'one among them'. The thought that she would have to leave the country that did not own her and go to a new one far away, scared her. As days went by, Shanti continued to be her best self in the orphanage. She noticed a change in how people looked at her now. Anxious with the developments in her life, she understood the pain of her friends who would be left behind until fate found them a new home.

Finally, the day had come. When the plane took off, she looked down at the busy city. She saw that the plane's shadow trailed on the ground but could not touch the aircraft. Likewise, she realized that the impurity and shame associated with her past would have no bearing in her new world.

In the company of her new parents, she felt pure for the first time in her life. She turned towards her mother and hugged her. Overwhelmed with their daughter's act of accepting them, the parents caressed their daughter tenderly.

"Thank you," she said sincerely and snuggled tight.

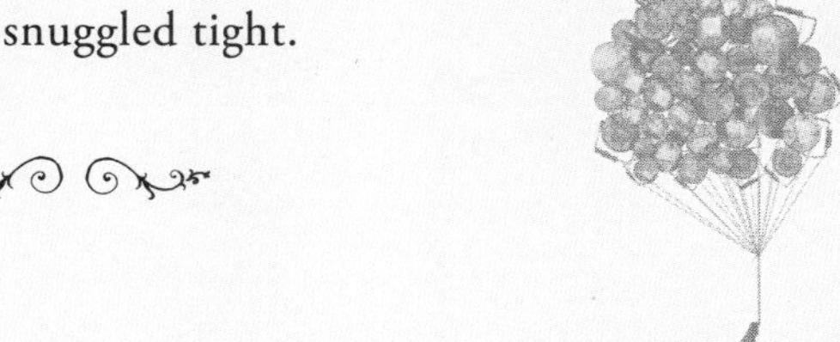

The Virat Mahabhuta

T

Trust

in dreams, for in them
is hidden the gate
to eternity.
Khalil Gibran

/trʌst/ firm belief in the reliability, truth, or ability of someone or something

A B C D E F G H I J K L M N O P Q R S **T** U V W X Y Z

TRUST

I am a pious man, a self-proclaimed one, and I have always believed in God. My belief is reaffirmed from time to time when He shows up in my life. I can recall several occasions, when He made his presence felt.

The incident narrated in this story unfolded a few years ago, when I was in doubt about a business deal and sought His counsel. You see, I often resort to an audience with Him when I have my doubts. I wished to take an idea to the market and was looking for investors to fund and help me. Eventually one, seemingly like-minded and wealthy investor agreed to fund the idea.

I was wary of borrowing money though, as any astute businessman should be, therefore I diligently considered the risks of having an investor on-board. I consulted professionals and learnt from books and blogs to clear my head. At each step, there was increasing clarity; however, I couldn't fully escape the muddle of doubts floating in my head. I hoped for His counsel on whether the new partnership would be blessed or not.

There was no sign from Him. Days turned to weeks. I waited, as any patient disciple would, for validation from Him before I could commit to an all eager-and-raring-to-go investor.

One evening, after I was charged with an energising run on the beach, I stopped to catch my breath. I felt a bit uncomfortable—a feeling of being watched pervaded me. Sure enough I noticed a fakir nearby with his eyes fixated on me. This unkempt, loony and a bit spooky fakir, dressed in a tattered black robe, was no more than ten yards away. Those of you not familiar with Mumbai should be warned judiciously, of the aspiring and ambitious actors who wander on Juhu beach looking for gullible preys to try their dramatic skills on. Considering the fakir to be one of this kind, I ignored him. However, when I noticed the fakir approaching me, his eyes locked with mine, I lost the rhythm in my breath again.

The fakir, barely two arms away now, made a one-on-one encounter unavoidable.

I assumed the poor soul needed some money to get a square meal for the day, therefore I quickly searched my pockets for odd change.

"Don't get into the partnership. Walk away before it is late!" the fakir bellowed dramatically, his hands stretched upwards and fingers pointing to the sky.

I was stunned, shocked and silenced. How in the world did this wretched fakir know! I was confused and pretended I hadn't heard him. He, as if aware of my pretence, bellowed again. By now, an audience had stopped to see the show, of which I had no desire or inclination to be part of. I got goose bumps and continued pretending that the fakir was not addressing to me.

Part awkward, part terrified, I shivered as I took out a ten rupee note, and offered it to the fakir, in the hope that he would take it and end the theatrics. But the fakir did not seem content. He continued to offer the same unsolicited advice on not venturing into any business with the investor. I was at a loss of words and felt numbness creeping up my legs. How could a fakir know about my thoughts... It was bizarre!

While I was still recuperating from the embarrassment, the fakir grabbed my hand and gave me a fifty rupee note in return. He came close and whispered in my ear, "May this serve your greed and end your pursuit!" He then walked away, shadowed by the massive crowd.

When I returned home, my wife sensed that I wasn't quite myself. I narrated the incident, hesitantly, to her. To my satisfaction, she too found it equally bizarre. We agreed to calm down and ignore the incident as a fabulous performance by some struggling artist and the context could be purely coincidental.

A few months passed and the new venture went bust. The investor turned out to be a suave swindler with a proven record of fraudulent dealings.

In hindsight, I believe God had shown up that day and advised me well.

I should have trusted the fakir!

The more you like yourself, the less
you are like anyone else,
which makes you

unique.

Walt Disney

/ juːˈniːk/ being the only one of its kind; unlike anything else

A B C D E F G H I J K L M N O P Q R S T **U** V W X Y Z

Akaar was different. And he knew it.

At play, he was forever among the cheerers. On the school bus, he was made to sit next to the bus caretaker. Neither invited to birthday parties nor included in school plays, Akaar spent his time at home drawing and colouring endlessly. He always had to sit in the middle of the front row in his class. They said he was a special child. He was autistic, to be specific.

Akaar always felt the pain of being alone, of being left out and the stigma of being different. He tried to be like the people he saw around him but it just wouldn't happen. He had reluctantly accepted his isolation as inevitable.

One day, the school announced a drawing competition as part of the annual day celebration. The guest of honour at the event, celebrity footballer Nessi—an alumnus of the school, was to select the best drawing from the submitted entries. This came easy to Akaar—the use of colours and pencils to bring a picture to life. So, he was thrilled. Other students too were delighted to know who the judge was! Groups were quickly formed and long discussions ensued about who would be drawing what. Akaar, as usual, was not part of any such group. It was tacitly assumed that it was best to leave him on his own.

On the Annual Day, all submissions were put squarely on display. The school had a lively atmosphere. Students admired each other's efforts yet each of them secretly hoped that Nessi would select their art. Akaar was no different. On seeing his drawing, the art teacher stood mesmerised. "Akaar, you have a gift that must be nurtured," he said encouragingly.

By the time Nessi arrived, the school had started to buzz like a swarm of bees. Suddenly, there was a flurry of activity. The press jostled to get the perfect shot and the students strained their necks and toes to catch a glimpse of him. The principal of the school stood with a taut smile as the air reverberated with adulatory screams of "Nessi, Nessi!" The talented footballer walked through the school corridor into the auditorium and comfortably sat through the speeches of the other dignitaries. Finally, when Nessi went onstage to declare the winning art, he narrated a lesser known story about his own childhood.

“When I was young, like you all are now, I was often sidelined by my peers for being different. They weren’t completely wrong about it—I was born an autistic child afterall. But, I did not brood or get upset about it because I had realized early in my life that my autism gave me some special powers too. I could focus on any idea intently and remain focussed on it for a very long time. Therefore, I persisted with keen focus on ideas that I loved deeply in my heart. My condition did surely make me different but it also made me unique. In retrospect, I believe my autism made me who I am today. It taught me that although each of us is different, yet all of us are unique in our own way.” He paused for a while and then resumed, “The painting that I am choosing today is one I resonate with deeply and completely because it is truly unique.” Nessi then lifted the veil that covered the winning art.

It was Akaar’s work that had been chosen. He was not just a special child; he was unique! That day, he found validation for his being. The audience gave a standing ovation to the winner. They agreed that being special made him unique.

V

Valour

is stability, not of legs and arms, but of courage and the soul.
Michel de Montaigne

/ˈvæl.ər/ great courage in the face of danger

A B C D E F G H I J K L M N O P Q R S T U **V** W X Y Z

VALOUR

"But Papa, I already know that Abhimanyu finally breaks into the *chakravyuh*. You have told me the story umpteen times!" Abhimanyu protested. "Here is the deal. Today I am going to tell you an original story of valour," he smiled at his father.

Arjun was all ears now. His son had grown up to be a smart boy. Abhimanyu was going to be in a hostel for the next three years, away from his parents for the first time, to pursue a graduation programme. As the father-son duo got ready for the overnight bus ride to Abhimanyu's college, Arjun continued to worry about his son.

The bus started and the journey had begun. Abhimanyu began narrating the story after the duo had made themselves comfortable in their seats.

"The night was stormy. The wind blew hard and incessant rain crashed against the window panes. The moment of being blessed with a child had come. It was becoming increasingly difficult for Arjun to take his pregnant wife Subhadra to the hospital. Married for eight years and still without a child, Arjun and Subhadra were anxious, worried and helpless."

"Their desire for a child had taken them to many temples and hospitals. The struggle had been long, but in the end, In Vitro Fertilisation (IVF) blessed them. Science often fills the loopholes that God cannot, and vice versa."

"Life had never been easy for Arjun. His Gods were seldom by his side. Will the rains stop? Will Gods help him? While it had seemed They wouldn't, Arjun somehow convinced a *rickshaw wala* and helped Subhadra get into it."

"They were about a furlong away from the hospital when the front wheel of the rickshaw got stuck in a pothole. Subhadra's labour was getting intense. By then her waters had broken and she was in terrible pain. Arjun lifted her in his arms and waded through deep potholes to finally reach the hospital. At the hospital's entrance, he fell to his knees and begged for help.

"Subhadra was wheeled through the corridors of the hospital and into the operation theatre. She was losing consciousness. The on-duty doctor told Arjun that Subhadra would have to undergo an emergency procedure to save their lives —her's and the baby's. Arjun was dizzy with cold and anxiety. His life seemed like a trap he constantly struggled to escape from. He felt he was in a *chakravyuh* with no escape. He consented. He had no choice."

"Arjun prayed to all his Gods, pleading with them to be kind to him that day. An hour later, the doctor came out of the operation theatre and congratulated Arjun with a smile, 'You are blessed with a baby boy!'"

"Arjun met his son later that night. It had been a long time since Arjun last experienced joy. He had forgotten what true happiness felt like. Looking at the baby, Arjun said to his wife, 'Subhadra... our son has come into the *chakravyuh* of life! He is our Abhimanyu."

Abhimanyu continued, "Papa, while most would be apprehensive, Abhimanyu liked being in the *chakravyuh*." He philosophised, "We all know that nobody gets out of the maze alive. But unlike everyone else, Abhimanyu knows best how to stand his ground, while he is in it. He is not afraid. He was born to break the *chakravyuh*."

The bus had picked up speed. It was now rolling on a dark salubrious woody road, far from the cemented labyrinthine town in the horizon. A pleasant nip filled the moonlit air. Abhimanyu was in deep sleep, swayed gently by the moving bus. Arjun slept much later. He began feeling confident for his son.

The next morning, as Abhimanyu bid farewell to Arjun, he assured his father comfortingly, "Papa, I will be fine in the hostel." Then he smiled mischievously and concluded, "Abhimanyu, son of Subhadra and Arjun, knows his way through any maze."

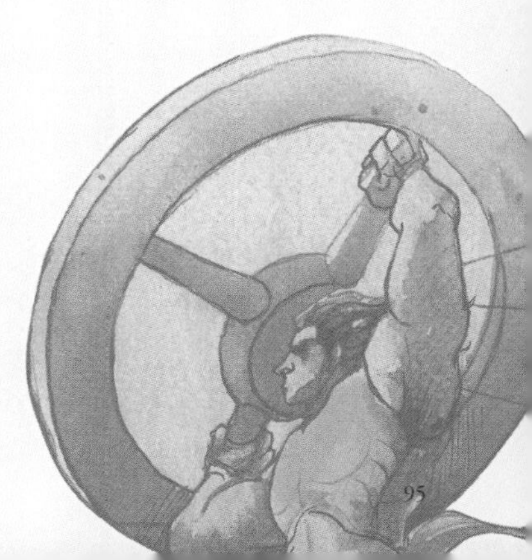

Wisdom is the supreme part of happiness

Wisdom

is the supreme part of happiness.
Sophocles

/ˈwɪz.dəm/ the quality of having experience, knowledge, and good judgement

A B C D E F G H I J K L M N O P Q R S T U V **W** X Y Z

WISDOM

Hushed murmurs erupted in the courtroom when the chieftain was produced in front of the judge.

"I can hold you in contempt of court!" the judge said. "Why aren't you dressed civilly?"

The people in the courtroom burst into laughter at the judge's remark. A few stray comments mocked the chieftain, who was wearing no more than a loin cloth. His headgear was an assemblage of feathers and his necklace was made of pebbles found on river beds. His face and body was smeared with ash, and his eyes looked large with an abundance of black soot applied around it.

The chieftain listened with a stoic expression as an interpreter translated the judge's words for him. His eyes were fixed on the painting hanging behind the judge's seat. The painting showed a large valley dotted with huts and a river flowing through it. Children were playing around these huts. Men and women were seen tending to the animals and the land. Their skin colour and garb was similar to that of the chieftain's.

"Will you speak or shall I sentence you to the gallows!" the judge commanded. More laughs erupted in the courtroom and filled the air with mockery. A voice boomed, "Order, order!"

The chieftain started speaking in a slow murmur and the interpreter translated it.

"I am the last son of the great Chief of the Wild. We have lived in this land for as long as man has lived. My people welcomed your people to live on this land, when you came famished from the north 200 winters ago. We tended your troubled souls. We gave you shelter, food and our women too. We gave your people health and life. We welcomed you as brothers."

"When more of your people came, they got guns with them. My grandfather did not like that. Your people killed my people and hanged them till their bodies rotted. Your people drove us out of our own land. When we fought back, your people killed more of us."

The chieftain's voice rose a notch. "Cornered and ashamed, my father let your people take our land on condition that you would let us live in peace. I am the only one living of the pure blood. My daughter, six years of age, died thirteen moons back. I wish is to bury her in the land of her forefathers. I wish to seed a plant over her buried body. My dead girl will live in the tree that will grow through her. That's my people's belief. But your people made laws that annexed our lands that now forbid me onto my own land. A car factory stands there on my people's land. They do not allow me to bury my little dead girl in the land of her ancestors. She is the among the last of my blood. When I die, there will be no more of my people to bury me."

The chieftain's voice now quavered. "Your people said you all are fair in word and spirit. Between me and my daughter, there stands your Law and your Wisdom. I hope you choose well."

The judge looked intently, his eyebrows raised, at the chieftain for a few long seconds and then adjourned the court for a few hours. As hushed murmurs filled the courtroom, people who walked close to the chieftain were either amazed or appalled to see such an unusual being not fit to be called human in their opinion.

The courtroom fell silent when the judge returned from his chamber. He read out his verdict: "By the authority vested in me by the laws of the white man, I order the state to immediately escort the Chief of the Wild to the land of his forefathers without delay, and provide all assistance necessary to lay his dead girl in her grave as per the beliefs and customs of his people. May the little girl of the honourable chief come back to life as a tree and live forever in her land. This court is dismissed."

That day, the wisdom with which the laws are made prevailed over the interpretation of the written text that defines it.

Find it because it is within you.

/ɛks/ denoting an unknown or unspecified person or thing

A B C D E F G H I J K L M N O P Q R S T U V W **X** Y Z

X - THE UNKNOWN

Some stories are better written than read. Write your story here.

Youth
has no age.
Pablo Picasso

/juːθ/ the period between childhood and adult age

A B C D E F G H I J K L M N O P Q R S T U V W X **Y** Z

YOUTH

"Dadi, aren't you too old to go on this trek?" Kiu, the granddaughter, asked curiously.

Dadi smiled. Her age was the last thing on her mind, however Kiu's question set her thinking. Since she lived in the village, she had missed spending time with her granddaughter. She was in the city now to join the group of young trekkers headed for the Himalayas. She wished to tell Kiu many things. She wondered where to begin. At eighty two, she had been through most of what life could offer. Five year old Kiu's journey had just begun. Dadi wished to tell her everything about getting old.

She started her monologue with her childhood: "When I was your age, I used to run to catch the rainbows. I never caught one, but I loved to run nevertheless. I would run hither and thither. One day while running, I tripped and fell off the roof of your great-grandfather's house and broke my left leg. My foot was in plaster for two long months. It was only after six months that I started playing again. My leg got better and better. Tsssh! How I miss running on the river banks. I used to race with the ducks! Mogli, the village mongrel, always gave me company. When it had pups, they all also ran with me, though not as fast."

"It was on the shallow river banks where I first saw the dancing girls. I joined them against the wishes of my grandfather. He said dancing is for the nautankis. But my father never said anything. Neither 'yes' nor 'no'. I used to dance for hours every day—Kathak. Not many girls appreciate Kathak these days. Dance is no longer taught with the same discipline as it used to be taught in my time. I lost touch with dancing after joining college. It just happened. By then my father wanted me to continue with Kathak, but the daily commute to college left me with no energy to practice. Besides, grandfather had never liked it."

At this point, Dadi bent to see if Kiu was asleep. Kiu was still listening, therefore Dadi continued, "Soon after, I fell in love with cycling. Do you know Kiu, that I was the fastest on my cycle? I rode to college in less than two hours from my village, always in time for the first class. By the time I finished college, I was married to your Dada. Your Dada had a large farm. He worked hard in the fields. I started helping him there. I liked standing with my feet in the wet paddy. I still do. At times, I could feel small fish nibbling at my feet and it felt ticklish. Your Dada and I used to laugh a lot while in the fields. These days you get everything in the market. We used to grow most of what we ate."

"I used to walk your Maa to school. In the evening, we would play. When your Mumma grew up to be as big as you are now, we used to hold each other's hands and do merry-go-rounds. She is a very good girl. I still want to play merry-go-rounds with her. When your Maa met your Papa, she left the village and came to this city. Without her, my life gradually became sedentary. Your Maa was the youngest of my six children. All of them left the village one by one. Your Dada also went to the heavens. With no one to play with, I sat idle most of the days, wondering what to do. Around that time I started to trek."

Dadi noticed that Kiu had begun to drool. She continued her monologue, "Every night, I dream of trekking up the big Himalayas. I also dream of going on walks with you. The city river is filthy. I will take you to the river in our village. I will also teach you how to run and how to sow paddy. You must also learn Kathak. I will take you to school and to the park - the one that has swings and slides. I will teach you to cycle. It is good to be on one's feet. It is good to be young. There is never a risk too huge or an age too old to enjoy the pleasures of life. No, it is not dangerous at all to scale Everest at my age."

Dadi realised that Kiu was cosily sleeping near her feet. She bent down and whispered in her ear, "I have learnt one thing really well in my life. Do you want to know what that is?"

"Youth has no age," she softly revealed with a smile.

Zeal

will do more than knowledge.

William Hazlitt

/zi:l/ great energy or enthusiasm in pursuit of a cause or an objective

A B C D E F G H I J K L M N O P Q R S T U V W X Y **Z**

ZEAL

The newly elected minister announced, "This village will prosper. A dam in the river will ensure not just electricity but water and livelihood all year round." The bored villagers clapped wryly whenever prompted by the minister's henchman. The hot, dry air of the lazy summer afternoon in the parched village was abuzz with innumerable flies and associated ailments. The villagers were tired both from sickness and from the many promises made to them several times earlier. They listened to the minister's words sceptically.

The chief of the village was however thrilled. The parched land had claimed many lives, including his son's. He was reminded of the dry summers when his mother had to feed the family, rotis made from dried grass. The chief had survived those droughts, but his three brothers and his only son were not as lucky. "No more hunger. No more deaths. Together we progress," the chief rallied zealously. He believed in every chance that the village was promised.

The chief lived in a thatched hut by the river with his granddaughter. His wife and daughter-in-law had also succumbed to hardships brought by the vagaries of nature. That evening when he told her about the dam, he saw a twinkle in the granddaughter's eyes. The little one was thrilled and unleashed a barrage of questions, most of which were beyond her grandfather's understanding. Her curiosity triggered the enthusiasm to know everything about a future where water was enough all through the year.

The new minister was true to his word. The construction of the dam began immediately. Overnight, the once neglected village turned into a busy, bustling junction. Villagers, who for generations prided in being farmers, took to being masons on the chief's behest. Those who tilled the land now excavated it while those who could drive tractors now drove trucks. There was hope that led many villagers to participate in the drive. There were doubts too, but the chief continued to rally for development. The environmentalists had warned the villagers about the dangers and harms the dam could bring. They reasoned that wherever a dam had been constructed, it had been detrimental to the local population and had led to the destruction of the natural ecosystem. The chief counter-reasoned against such propaganda and argued that wherever the dams had not been built, there had been poverty, starvation and deaths. The village had seen enough of it already; therefore, slowly but surely, everyone aligned and the dam was bound to be a reality. The voices against the development of the dam were silenced, if not by reason then by the sheer size of the dominant coalition of villagers that the chief had managed to put together.

A vertical wall-like structure started coming up. The chief's granddaughter would run up to the top of the hill to see the magical structure come up rock by rock and brick by brick. Finally, it was the day of the inauguration. It was a historic day. The villagers—adults and children alike, paced to the top of the mountain. Amidst cheers and claps, the villagers welcomed the Prime Minister of the nation, who had specially come to inaugurate the dam. At the end of a countdown, the Prime Minister had to press a button to detonate a series of bombs. The detonations would clear the big boulders and create a new path, altering the river's course towards the dam.

The villagers had not seen anything like this before. A lake had started to build up in the gorge that separated the mountains. The water of this lake could be harnessed to irrigate agricultural lands, create electricity, and nurture many dreams. The cheers and claps grew louder with the rising level of water. The villagers were both scared and happy at the same time. With hearts heavy from memories of their ancestors, they saw their land submerge—their homes now buried underneath the new lake.

The chief watched vigilantly with his eyes, now moist. He was taken back to the days when his father would get ready every morning to find water for the withering crops. He saw himself as a child climbing on to a dried tree in hope of some fruit. He imagined his brothers and son tilling the parched fields. He saw his mother and wife packing the harvest in bags hoping that they had enough for the whole year to live by.

The chief turned towards the villagers. He raised his fist and cheered, "No more hunger. No more deaths. Together we progress!" The villagers joined him in the sloganeering, this time convinced beyond any doubt, of a prosperous future.

the wow people!

A | Alishka Varde Singh

B | Devashish Makhija

C | Bijit Kundu

D | Late Krsna Ananda

E | Ruchi Bakshi Sharma

F | Bimal Poddar

G | Anoop Patnaik

H | Kapil Sharma

I | Kriti Monga

J | Archan Nair

K | Rajesh Soni

L | Allen Shaw

M | Nitin Patel

N | Prashant Miranda

O | Sunaina Sadarangani Gera

P | Rajashree Basu Kundu

Q | Ashdeen Z. Lilaowala

R | Anuj Sharma

S | Rajat Nagpal

T | Kavita Singh Kale

U | Pradipta Ray

V | Prasun Basu

W | Sucharita Sengupta Suri

X | Amit Ashar

Y | Priya Kuriyan

Z | Shweta Mohapatra

✒ | Amit Suri

A
B
C
D
E
F
G
H
I
J
K
L
M
N
O
P
Q
R
S
T
U
V
W
X
Y
Z
THE
WOW
TEAM

ATTITUDE by Alishka Varde Singh | Rabid Crafter, Party Stylist, YouTuber
f /DIYDAYwithAlishka | **f** /happypeople.in

Alishka loves working with paper & fabric and making new things from a bunch of random craft supplies. Party styling and her videos happened as an offshoot of her love for DIY. She also loves sketching... it's like meditation to her.

Medium & Size: Pencil Sketch / 18″ x 12″

From the Artist's Eye: At first all I could picture for the word Attitude was a very confident woman in snazzy sunglasses not caring what the world thinks. I even made a few sketches till I realised that that's really not what attitude is, it's what we've been made to believe.

An attitude is a very strong, deep, secure feeling you have in your heart that makes you do things you didn't think you could. So when I read the associated quote, it clicked for me. A little something, if we give positivity to it, can really make a huge difference. And so I sketched again. Flowers are my thing—it started with a little girl watering her small flower and it then blooms and blooms into gorgeous large flowers with my favourite intricate patterns in them!

BALANCE by Devashish Makhija | Writer, Filmmaker, Graphic Poet
imdb.com/name/nm1941973

His parents gave Devashish his name. Pure chance gave him his nationality. No one asked him if he wanted the religion he got. The system gave him an education. And then proceeded to make it null and void. The only thing he got to choose in his life are his words. So he likes to choose them carefully.

Medium & Size: Computer Graphics / 18″ x 12″

From the Artist's Eye: In the piece '750mm', the 'system' fails the 'individual' yet again. It starts raining in a seaside city that had promised its citizens there will be no waterlogging. Even though the water is rising, the Meteorological Department has promised that it won't rise above 750 mm. This piece is the first person perspective of a shanty-dweller, who, when he sits on his haunches, is exactly 750mm high. He sits outside his destroyed home as the water rises, immersing him, taking his life slowly. He does this to prove the Meteorological Department wrong. He also does this to show he can 'hold on', yet 'let go'. He doesn't manage to change the 'system'. He doesn't become a 'martyr'. Like all others of his kind, he becomes a footnote in yet another media story. He is not missed by what we call Mother India (which ends up being nothing more than just another genderless monstrous machinery).

CURIOSITY by Bijit Kundu | Animator, Illustrator, Biker, Scuba diver
f/Johnny-Soko-and-the-Flying-Robots-Design-Pvt-Ltd-274707785919466

Bijit's Sunday off-roading adventures out in the wild, help fuel his imagination and keep him going through all the challenges in life.

Medium & Size: Pencil sketch / 12″ x 18″

From the Artist's Eye: Curiosity is a feeling of inquisitiveness, mixed with anxiety and fear, which ignites our wildest imagination. It does not stop at one single thing or discovery; it keeps on going forward, it has its own offshoots. Events keep on linking with each other which leading to newer knowledge. It is like a maze, and when we come to the end of the tunnel, we see a newer light which we did not know existed before. This gives us immense joy. From curiosity comes new knowledge. My artwork depicts this sense of anticipation and the exciting imaginary journey while going through the maze of the unknown.

DILIGENCE by Late Krsna Ananda | Mixed Media Artist
joydatta.carbonmade.com | **Bē** /joydatta | **f** /joydatta74

Late Krsna Ananda aka Joy Datta was inspired by everything around him, although it did get amusing for him when they appeared in rectangles. He was always aspiring to test the bounds of reality in a woven and created world. You could count on Joy for an out-of-the-box frame.

Medium & Size: Photography and Phone App / 7.8″ x 8.3″

From the Artist's Eye: The image is from a series of mirrorgrams which I have been shooting for over 2 years. I chose this image from a *Vat Purnima* celebration where women tie holy threads by wishing and vowing for the health and prosperity of their near and dear ones. The Peepal tree represents the tree of life and is sacred in the Hindu religion. It supports life of all sorts and is famous for its long life. The Peepal tree also has the property to purify air. The cotton thread is just the opposite. It represents the fragile nature of life, love, trust, faith, and all things that go on to make up a relationship. A single thread may be weak, but, when it is wound 108 times around the trunk, it becomes strong. It is no longer so fragile and no longer easy to break.

EMPATHY by Ruchi Bakshi Sharma | Artist, Filmmaker, Toymaker
www.ruchibakshisharma.com | /_airdrome_

Ruchi studied Communication Design and has several award winning live action and stop motion shorts to her credit. Her picaresque characters, often based on outlandish folklore and equipped with supernatural powers, seem to inhabit a strange and wonderful world of myth and fancy.

Medium & Size: Pencil & Computer Graphics / 18″ x 12″

From the Artist's Eye: Verdant growth envelopes a girl in her mind garden. She, and the reflection that represents her are entangled through loops of time and space. Everything mirrors here. Her mind is still as she attunes to a resonating transference taking place in her heart. Her eyes are closed as she concentrates on expansion. When her guiding forces begin to take form, the past and the future collapse, the quality of empathy is engaged and a hidden perception begins to flow along.

FREEDOM by Bimal Poddar | Animator, Illustrator
fairycows.co.in | f /fairycows

Born in West Bengal, Bimal never played football. He went to Ahmedabad for studies but didn't try his hand at dandia either. Currently living in Mumbai, he is tackling challenges with his visual and creative skills. In between, he founded the Fairycows Animation studio.

Medium & Size: Pencil & Computer Graphics / 18″ x 12″

From the Artist's Eye: Freedom is like the breeze on a day when the moon shines bright; an old envelope for a letter sent that is now lost; an unravelled secret; wavy, hasty hair; the glitter on a shiny contour. Freedom is space unobstructed, unrestricted. It is your breath and mine.

GOODNESS by Anoop Patnaik | Graphic Designer
designstack.com

Anoop lives in Mumbai and is the co-founder of Design Stack, a branding and graphic design studio. He believes in minimalism, which reflects in his personality; he can often be found expressing himself in less words but more smiles.

Medium & Size: Computer Graphics / 8″ x 12″

From the Artist's Eye: For the word Goodness, I drew inspiration from a line in Cormac McCarthy's The Road. In this tale of a father and son's journey together, and at a point when it is almost certain that the two are going to be separated forever, the father alleviates his son's anxiety about getting lost in the big, bad world with the words, "Goodness will find the little boy. It always has. It will again." The line suggests that 'goodness' is, in a sense, distilled from the key ingredients of the state of childhood—innocence, instinct, hope and optimism.

The thought contained in this line immediately triggered off a comic book / graphic novel-style approach in my head. In my interpretation, boyhood is a somewhat superheroic state, with a hyper-instinct for goodness. Though the young character is not an embodiment of goodness himself, he can, with his hyper-instinct, manipulate the existing sources and draw that goodness within himself, particularly in moments of crisis.

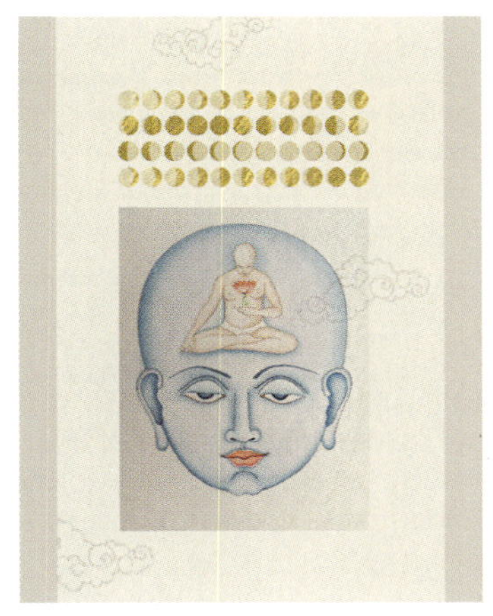

HONESTY by Kapil Sharma | Graphic Designer and Visual Artist
studiofunc.com | f /studiofunc | /studiofunc |
t kapilsharma.tumblr.com

Kapil, the sixth artist in the family, is based in Udaipur, Rajasthan. His work fuses his long lasting interest in the literary and painterly conventions of Nathdwara miniatures, with his other passion; documenting nature and the city's built fabric. This astonishing blend has resulted in a work which re-contextualises the narratives of the Nathdwara miniatures in a contemporary manner, thus, making it more accessible to the public. His works are a part of several private collections and museums all over the world.

Medium & Size: Mixed Media / 12″ x 18″

From the Artist's Eye: Sitting quietly, I turn within. I am a point of light...I am a soul. In this awareness of I, the soul, I emerge from within my own being, the quality of peace and honesty. When we are not honest with others, we are not being honest with ourselves. One's own personal truth relates to the universal truth. Honesty is living from the truth of your being, loving yourself, your needs, desires and life. It is more important to be remembered for your honesty and good deeds than any other thing. Let the lotus flower bloom within yourself!

INTEGRITY by Kriti Monga | Graphic Designer, Illustrator, Hand lettering & Visual Artist
turmericdesign.com | /kritimonga_ | /kritimonga |
/turmericdesign | /turmericdesignstudio

Kriti has an obsession for all things type- and hand-crafted. She tinkers with lettering, typography, words and meaning in all sorts of ways; draws travel and sketchnote diaries, teaches occasionally, and goes wandering off in foreign lands whenever she can get away.

Medium & Size: Hand embroidery on fabric / 8″ x 12″

From the Artist's Eye: Integrity means consistent action towards one's values, even when immensely difficult, or as the quote says, 'when no one is looking'. This is aptly represented by the flourishing of a healthy, happy tree, due to the persistent efforts of its roots that themselves remain unseen underground.
The painstaking needlework symbolises consistent, meaningful action, creating a pointillism-inspired soil that the hand-lettered 'roots' have burrowed their way through.

JOY by Archan Nair | Visual Artist, Illustrator, Digital Artist
archann.net | /archann

Archan is a self-taught artist specialising in mixed media, illustration, and digital art. His visual expressions are part of a journey which is deeply influenced by the mysteries of our existence and how every action, emotion, and our interconnectedness in a universal scale sets off a chain of reactions, which we experience from the micro to the macro scale.

Medium & Size: Digital Art and Illustration / 12″ x 13″

From the Artist's Eye: The thought behind this artwork is to realise the true self—that we are the infinite, undivided being, the untouched awareness, which embraces all in its love; that there is no separation between anything in creation, that our true nature is happiness and joy.

KINDNESS by Rajesh Soni | Artist
f /galleryone2008 | /rajeshsoniudaipur

Rajesh has become known primarily for his abilities to sketch street life and old heritage havelis, and hand colouring black and white photos. He is the son of artist Lalit Soni, and grandson of Prabhu Lal Soni, who was once the court photographer to the Maharana Shree Bhopal Singh of Mewar. Rajesh lives in Udaipur, Rajasthan.

Medium & Size: Oil on canvas / 13″ x 9″

From the Artist's Eye: Since childhood, I have seen the people who are depicted in my art. I love the way they come and play music. For me, they are the best examples of how one can spread kindness and happiness in the lives of others without expecting anything in return.

LOVE by Allen Shaw | Artist, Illustrator and Storyteller
allenshaw.com | f /allen.shaw.716195 | /theolddrifter

Allen is an Indian based in Berlin. His life revolves around travelling and recording his journeys in his sketchbooks. Travelling and sketching are the means to feeding his gypsy soul.

Medium & Size: Watercolour & a lot of love on paper / 12″ x 18″

From the Artist's Eye: It is already a good start when you get 'love' as the word to illustrate. Nudity, illusion, magic, flight and the 'Holy Dove' were some of the words that kept circling in my head while thinking of 'love'. At some stage, I let the watercolours take over. The style used in this artwork is the result of an ongoing series of experiments with watercolours.

MODESTY by Nitin Patel | Artist
f /nitinpatelart

Nitin started as an exhibition designer but his interests drifted him to the world of computer graphics. He is a self-taught computer graphics artist and loves to learn and explore new media and art forms. He is currently mastering the use of watercolours, which is reflected in his recent work.

Medium & Size: Digital Painting / 12″ x 18′

From the Artist's Eye: When I had the word 'modesty' assigned to me, the first thing that came to my mind was an iceberg. What we see at the surface is only the partial truth about the iceberg—the bulk of whose form lies hidden. The forms in my art, too, are derived from the physical appearance of the iceberg. Ingrained in the artwork is a play of hues where I have tried to intuitively highlight the emotional qualities that are associated with the word.

NAIVETY by Prashant Miranda | Artist, Animator, Scribe
prashart.blogspot.com | /prashola | f /Prashant Miranda

Prashant oscillates between Canada and India where he documents his life in watercolour journals, murals, children's books and films.

Medium & Size: Watercolour & Pen / 15″ x 9″

From the Artist's Eye: For my word 'naivety', I had to keep my artwork whimsical. I started with splotches and splashes of colour, not knowing what was going to come out eventually. However, I trusted the fact that it would certainly lead to an outcome, despite not having a clue of what the process would be. I also drew inspiration from the line, 'naivety is the first truth of aesthetics', and approached it with the most frivolous beginning that led to my final artwork.

OM by Sunaina Sadarangani Gera | Artist, Cake Artist
⊛ sunaina.in | **f** /sunainatheartist | **f** /sweetcoutureforyou

Sunaina was born into a Sindhi family in the island of Curacao and raised in Nigeria and India. The artist had exposure to different cultures very early in life, which helped define her unique style. She concentrates on imaginative compositions and figure drawings, which are brought to life with the powerful and bold use of colours. Working primarily with acrylics, she uses a palette knife in place of a brush, adding depth and weight to create a variety of textures.

Medium & Size: Acrylics on canvas / 24" x 36"

From the Artist's Eye: I am not religious but I am spiritual. I look for meaning in the everyday life, with a holistic approach to everything I do. I found the meaning of Om vary between different schools of theology. What does Om mean to me? What does the chanting of Om do for me? The quest resulted in this painting—Om (Shanti) which represents a lady who puts all her daily preoccupations aside and meditates on Om to connect with the universe, and soaks up on positive energy. The play of colours in the background represents the distractions of the everyday life. The flow of energy is depicted in fragments of white falling down from the universe.

PERSISTENCE by Rajashree Basu Kundu | Graphic Designer
⊛ johnnysoko.carbonmade.com |
⊛ johnnysokoandtheflyingrobots.com

Rajashree lives in Mumbai near the greens of the Sanjay Gandhi National Park. Botanical drawings and foliage are strong in her designs. She loves everything vintage and exotic. Her work ranges from designing identities, packaging, corporate communication and theme-based parties and events.

Medium & Size: Mix Media / 12" x 8"

From the Artist's Eye: For my visual representation of Persistence, I had to choose a subject which though being soft and naive at first sight, is revealed as a winner. So the idea of a soft plant with tendrils came to my mind. No matter how many obstacles you put in front, it somehow manages to outsmart, work around and come out in full bloom. It remains absolutely unaffected by fences or barbed wires. And while it grows, nature too, comes to help in a silent way in the form of birds and bees. Overall, it is a happy process, nothing to worry about. That is how anything meaningful grows. So, my artwork, though describing a painful process of growth, shows a happy and cheerful ambience, indicating how one must carry on regardless.

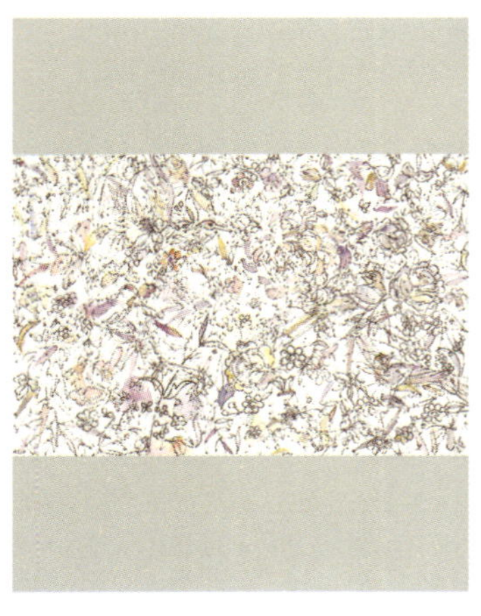

QUEST by Ashdeen Z. Lilaowala | Textile Designer, Author
ashdeen.com | f /ashdeen

Ashdeen specializes in Parsi Gara embroidery. In his creations, he beautifully amalgamates the ancient craft with his contemporary ideas.

Medium & Size: Watercolour with Pen on paper / 10″ x 15″

From the Artist's Eye: The idea was to achieve something difficult and yet make it look effortless. I have created the artwork by drawing with pen on thin fabric foam and allowing the ink to create impressions on paper. Multiple images have been used from my embroidery archive to create a mélange of textures and forms. Some of these forms have been highlighted with watercolour. The image makes you keep searching for new forms and narratives.

RESPECT by Anuj Sharma | Fashion Designer
f /buttonmasala | /@buttonmasala | /@anujsharmanid

Anuj sees without preconceived thoughts. He lets his mind speak. He trusts his instincts. He designs, writes and plays.

Medium & Size: Handkerchiefs, Mannequin and Thread

From the Artist's Eye: Every material, every tiny thing that exists in this world, exists for a purpose. The purpose might be small, but it completes everything around us. A handkerchief, for example, is the smallest fabric piece used and hardly gets any mention. But it does a lot. Everything we respect, whether small or big, will give us back for sure. Respect is not what we get; it is what we give. And it all comes back for sure.

SINCERITY by Rajat Nagpal | Storyteller beyond medium
in /in/rajatnagpalfilmaker | /user/nagpalandsinha |
/rrajat_photography/?hl=en

Rajat is best introduced as a polymath and serial entrepreneur. A pre-visualiser, producer, director of several award winning television commercials, music videos, corporate and documentary films and shorts, he has also written stories, screenplays and lyrics while dabbling with production design, costume design, music composition and cinematography. A Masterchef Season 2 finalist, he has co-founded the largest professional networking portal for the Indian creative industry. He lives in Goa and continues to dabble in multiple media.

Medium & Size: Photo Montage / 13″ x 12″

From the Artist's Eye: "Khalos-e-Baqa, Shiddhat-e-Jahaan; Raqs-e-Bismil, Rubaiyat Hai Yahaan."
My artwork is an ode to the persevering spirit of Mumbai and its people that pushes them to continue to perform beyond their known capacity, to put one foot before another and carry on.

Fourteen years ago, I met Mumbai for the first time. It was love at first sight. At the time, I may not have found it to be the most beautiful in the world but I certainly believe that it was the most alluring. Today, I am as much her as she is me. Mumbai, thus, is the grand city that personifies the spirit of survival, for me.

TRUST by Kavita Singh Kale | Transmedia Artist
/kavitasinghkale | vimeo.com/undergroundworm |
Bē /kavitasinghkale

Kavita is an award winning filmmaker, artist, author and illustrator. Traveling drives her thoughts. Being a part of new cultures, learning about them and translating it into visual poems, is what interests her. She is the co-founder of an interdisciplinary studio called Underground Worm Art & Design.

Medium & Size: Acrylic on canvas / 16″ x 20″

From the Artist's Eye: '*Virat Mahabhuta*' interprets elements of nature as demigods who are in conflict with monsters mutated from the by-products of human consumption. The series of narrative artworks describe a state of enigma, where battles between the two groups are undecided with the display of power struggle. Regardless of the final outcome, there is hope and trust that these forces of nature will overpower the evil through self-realization of humanity. If this does not happen, the forces will continue to heal themselves after a tough ordeal to create a new ecosystem completely alien to humans. Khalil Gibran's quote, "Trust in dreams, for in them is hidden the fate to eternity." inspired '*Virat Mahabhuta*'.

UNIQUE by Pradipta Ray | Animation, Filmmaker, Painter, Illustrator
vimeo.com/130744004 | f /pradipta.ray.12

Pradipta has been part of many acclaimed film projects—winning awards and appreciation. He is also a visiting faculty at National Institute of Design, Ahmedabad and perhaps the institute's first and only transgender professor widely popular with students and colleagues alike. Pradipta lives in Mumbai.

Medium and Size: Mixed Media / 12" x 18"

From the Artist's Eye: In my art, I have tried to depict that we need not wear masks to hide our true selves.

Masqueraded in masks
Forgets what lies beneath
Beneath lies the core
That is pure
The core that is true
The core that is you
The you that is unique

VALOUR by Prasun Basu | Animator, Installation Artist, Muralist, Madari
offish.co.in

Prasun qualifies to be an Animator, Artist, Sculptor, Designer, Animatronics Enthusiast and more because he just loves to handle pencil, paint, stylus, clay, fur, foam, fabric, silicon, latex and some other gooey, smelly stuff. Of late, he has been spending a lot of time with his 3D printer, soldering iron and tinkering with Arduinos, servo motors and radio controllers.

Medium & Size: Watercolour & Pen / 6" x 11.5"

From the Artist's Eye: My art is inspired by the brave sixteen-year-old Abhimanyu from the epic Mahabharata. He is the heroic representation of valour while fighting on the 13th day of the Kurukshetra war.

WISDOM by Sucharita Sengupta Suri | Graphic Designer, Visual Communicator
⊛ SeekRed.com | ⊛ twagaa.com

Sucharita's forte is in the understanding and usability of graphic & communication design tools for a wide variety of media. In personal life, other than loving a good sleep, she dabbles with many creative ideas like organising workshops with kids, crafting, photography and more.

Medium & Size: Watercolour & pen / 12″ x 12″

From the Artist's Eye: 'Happiness' and 'wisdom' to me are the conscious unending pursuits of attaining balance and harmony with all elements that surrounds us.

In my art, I have shown *Gyan Mudra* with the core elements—the Earth, Water, Air, Fire, Ether. The *Gyan Mudra* is a powerful *mudra* (or hand position) practised for thousands of years by yogis; it is known to bring peace, calm and spiritual progress. The balance of the core elements brings stability, love and joy.

X by Amit Ashar | Photographer
⊛ amitashar.com

Amit is based out of Mumbai. His style is minimalistic and his themes are poignant. His eye has a childlike curiosity which loves to capture 'The Phenomenal Magic of the Ordinary'—his ongoing personal body of work which is a unique and delightful way of seeing the everyday and ordinary around us.

Medium & Size: Camera Canon EOS 1ds mark 3 / 16″ x 11″

From the Artist's Eye: I feel that pictures and photographs are just about impossible to describe in words. Both have nothing to do with each other. This image is my reaction to one of the whispers and nudges that I get from the world around me. It is the magic in the ordinary. The interpretation is upto the viewer.

YOUTH by Priya Kuriyan | Animator, Illustrator, Comic Book Artist
priyakuriyan.blogspot.com | pkuriyan.blogspot.com |
t kuriyanmakeskomics.tumblr.com

Priya currently lives in New Delhi, and spends her time filling her sketchbooks with strange caricatures of its residents.

Medium & Size: Watercolour and pencil / 18″ x 12″

From the Artist's Eye: It is how we act, what we do and feel that makes us feel youthful and this is what I wanted to depict through this almost mirror image of a grandmother and her granddaughter. But, perhaps the younger girl is just an image of the older woman's soul, who knows!

ZEAL by Shweta Mohapatra | Visual Artist, Illustrator, Animation Filmmaker
/shwetamohapatrainsta | shwetamohapatra.blogspot.in

Shweta lives in Delhi with her architect husband and her son. She is always juggling multiple things and if you meet her she might look distracted, but actually she is keenly observing the world around her.

Medium & Size: Hand-drawn and digitally coloured / 12″ x 18″

From the Artist's Eye: The artwork here, represents my friend Navleen, who lives in the hills in Vashisth, Himachal Pradesh (India) along with her pet dog 'Rosa'. She is an artist, maker of various things, nature lover and a free-spirited individual full of *joie de vivre*. Her zeal in life has inspired me to make this artwork, I hope to capture her energy, her beautiful surroundings, her love for nature and animals through this illustration.

The WOW Project proves Aristotle right.

When people work together, the net result is greater than the individual contribution of its members.

Isn't this beautiful? Isn't this WOW?

Amit Suri
⊛ SeekRed.com | ⊛ twagaa.com

Amit is inspired by all things creative. Making small crafts, playing with words, exploring new places and being able to connect the dots successfully makes him happy.

more words of wonder

Of the many Words of Wonder, only 26 could be included in this book. Here are more words—may these inspire you to create beautiful art and write stories. I hope that you will share your creativity with me at *https://wow.twagaa.com/collaborate/* and soon, we will be ready with the second edition of *WOW - A to Z.*

A ability • abundance • acceptance • accountability • accuracy • achievement • acknowledgement • acting on convictions • activism • adaptability • adoration • adventure • advice • affection

B beauty • belief • benevolence • benignity • bliss • bravery

C candour • caring • caution • celebration • celibacy • certainty • chance • change • chaos • character • charity • charm • chastity • cheerfulness • chivalry • choice • citizenship

D decency • dedication • deliberation • delight • dependability • desire • destiny • detachment • determination • devotion • dignity • diligence • diplomacy

E eagerness • earnestness • ecstasy • education • efficiency • endurance • effort • elegance • elevation • eloquence • emotion • emptiness • encouragement • endurance

F fairness • faith • faithfulness • family • farsightedness • fearlessness • feeling • fidelity • flexibility • flow • focus • forbearance • foresight • forgiveness • fortitude

G gallantry • generosity • genius • gentleness • genuineness • glory • goals • godliness • grace • grandeur • gratefulness • gratitude • gravitas • gravity • growth

H happiness • harmlessness • harmony • healing • health • helpfulness • holiness • honour • hope • hospitality • humanity • humility • humour

I idealism • ideals • identities • illumination • imagination • impartiality • imperfection • inclusion • incorruptibility • independence • individuality

J joyfulness • judgment (good) • justice

K kinship • knowledge

L laughter • leadership • learning • leisure • liberalism • liberty • listening • logic • loyalty • luck • luxuriate

M majesty • management • manners • maturity • meaning • mellowness • mercy • mildness • mindfulness • mistakes

N niceness • nobility • non-covetousness • non-duality • non-separateness • non-violence • nostalgia • nurturance • nurturing

O obedience • objectivity • obligations • open-heartedness • open-mindedness • openness • optimism • order • orderliness • organization • originality

P pacifism • paradise • passion • patience • patriotism • peace • peacefulness • penitence • pensiveness • perseverance • personality • perspective • persuasion • philanthropy

Q quality

R radiance • rapture • rationality • realism • reality • realization • reason • rebirth • receptivity • reciprocity • reconciliation • rectitude • redemption • refinement • reflection • relaxation • release

S sacredness • sacrifice • sadness • salvation • sanity • satiety • satisfaction • secrecy • security • seeing • self-awareness • self-centeredness • self-confidence • self-control • self-discipline

T tactfulness • talent • taste • team-spirit • teamwork • temperance • tenacity • tenderness • thankfulness • thoroughness • thoughtfulness • thrift • time • tithing • tolerance

U unconditional love • understanding • unique • unity • universality • unselfishness

V values • verbal acuity • victory • vigour • virility • virtue • vision • vitality • vulnerability

W wealth • wholesomeness • will • wonder • work • workmanship • worship • worth

X X - the unknown

Y youthfulness

Z zealousness • zest

acknowledgements

Thank you Alishka, Devashish, Bijit, Ruchi, Bimal, Anoop, Kapil, Kriti, Archan, Rajesh, Allen, Nitin, Prashant, Sunaina, Rajashree, Ashdeen, Anuj, Rajat, Kavita, Pradipta, Prasun, Amit, Priya, Shweta and Joy (I know that you have taken birth again and are living a happy and blissful childhood somewhere). All of you are amazing people. I admire you all for the amazing creative work you do, which inspires many like me to do more and do that beautifully.

Thank you Atul Sethi, Ashok Bhattacharjee and Saira Kurup for your suggestions and edits.

Thank you Sucharita Suri and Anamika Srivastava for designing and putting the book together.

Thank you Megha Shah for proofing the book and for your valuable suggestions.

Thank you Rahul Seth for the sharp proofing of each story and suggesting valuable changes.

Thank you Garima Syal for the thorough edit and for valuable inputs in the stories.

Thank you Mannat Khanna for the final design tweaks.

Thank you Brajesh Kumar for doing more than believing.

Thank you Anuj Malhotra (Bahrisons Books) for being a mentor par excellence and to have appeared in the life of this book when needed most.

Thank you Papa, Mummy, Aashish and Dolly. You are God's invaluable gifts to me.

Thank you Vikramaditya and Inaira. Both of you are old enough to read this. May you soon grow up to know why I thank you for being in my life.

Thank you Sucharita for everything.

The meaning and pronounciation of the words from A-Z are taken from the Oxford English Dictionary.

* *Continued from page 6*

'seven hundred and fifty millimeters'

it must
have been about two dozen drums
being beaten elegant
in a marchpast

they were out of sync
being beaten out of shape
out of line

dull

scared

trying to say something
they knew i wouldn't like to hear

the sound felt far away

till i shut my eyes
and heard it on the roof

where a thousand raindrops knocked in syncopation
angry drummers
who wanted most
to cry

they were not the only ones

there were drummers on the floor inside
the ones that fell through
alice-holes in the roof

every drummer
one strike on the drum

every strike
a drop in the flood

i sat on blue haunches
motionless
on the threshold
the chief guest at the marchpast
couldn't muster a salute

the door too swollen
by dampness to shut

drops drummed on the road
level
in front of me
or the bits of it
that still thrust desperately
above the water

i heard them

only heard
as my eyes were getting lazy in the dark

it's strange
how god didn't think of electricity

without it
eyes have nothing to do
after the sun sets

drops drummed on the gathering
water

drops
drummed on metal

on wood

on plastic

on other drops

on me

drops jostled with drops
some lived a little longer
arcing in the
low howling wind

i felt some on my eye lids

i used my eyes for the other sense
of touch

i'd soon be using my hands to see with

the water
mostly a solution of urine
blood
oil and other nameless fluids
began by covering my toes

it was a queer sensation
a mix of dread and relief

i wiggled my digits
one against another
feeling them clean

another strange thing

how

when the flood gates in the skies
crack open
taps
at the ends of proud erect pipes
run dry

and howl like wind chased
when twisted open

we take them too much for granted

taps

the water crept up my ankle

calf

and back in the meantime
moving up faster than
my thoughts could descend

i couldn't hear the drummers
on the floor inside
behind me
anymore

there too drops drummed on water

now
a different depth
from that on the outside
before me

they hit different notes
the two

out of sync

out of shape

out of line

the water slid carefully
coldly
up around my chest

as my heart caught the drum beat
i thought i saw
float by

dr. alam's stethoscope

onions

an underwear

and a dead dog

it could have been a bitch

i'd call it a dog
the dead deserve respect

i felt my resolve weaken

but i had to be sure

when i sat down
doubled up on my haunches
sentinel
for my little world behind me
i was seven hundred and fifty
millimeters high, give or take
a few

the meteorological department
played drummers

thumping their backs
on getting an estimate right

six fifty it was
the last time they said
six fifty it will be
again

nothing to worry about
moderately heavy to slightly heavy

stay indoors they said

indoors

where you'd be safe
and dry they said

the water's been talking to me
for the last thirty eight hours

it's gotten past six fifty it says

it's drumming
on the highrise roofs of
the meteorologists it says

they can't hear the drummers
i can

the rain says i understand

and it swells up to my chin

it brings me all the smells of the city

the stale pav

the rotting eggs

the sulabh shauchalay
washed clean

finally
the diesel
that turned 40 paise dearer last week

the buffaloes that will never again
have ropes tied and tightened
around their necks

i smell with my eyes
as the water climbs over my nose

it has to be seven fifty

it's going to be more

i need to show them

i need to get up from here now

i need this rain to stop so i can go tell them

i need this cramp in my calves to let up

i have to get up

i need some light

i need some water i can drink

i need these crickets to stop chirping so loud

or i'll lose my hearing

just like them.

-Devashish Makhija

glossary

abhimanyu	a character from the ancient Indian epic, Mahabharata
amma	mother
baba	father
banyan tree	an Indian fig tree, whose branches produce wide-ranging aerial roots which later become accessory trunks
beta	son
chakravyuh	a multi-tiered defensive formation that looks like a blooming lotus or disc when viewed from the top
dada	grandfather
dadi	grandmother
dandiya	a traditional folk dance form of India
didi	older sister
diwali	an important Hindu festival, also called the festival of lights
fakir	a religious ascetic who lives solely on alms
gori memsahib	colloquial way of referring to a high-bred, fair complexioned lady
gyan mudra	a meditation gesture in yoga that promotes physical and mental health
haveli	a traditional mansion in South Asia, usually one with historical and architectural significance
janm bhoomi	place of birth
kathak	one of the eight major forms of Indian classical dance
kholi	small makeshift hut
kurukshetra	site of the battle in the Indian epic, Mahabharata

madari	a juggler
mahabharata	a major Sanskrit epic of ancient India
maharana	king
mantra	a word or syllable used repeatedly to attain desired results
nathdwara	an important Hindu temple town in India
nautankis	popular folk theatre performance generally seen in rural India
om shanti	greeting and parting salutation, where 'Om' (in Hinduism) is believed to be the sound of the universe and 'shanti' means peace
paayas	a popular Bengali sweet dish made with milk, rice and jaggery
papa	father
parsi gara	a type of saree with traditional embroidery worn in the Parsi community
peepal tree	a native deciduous tree that is considered sacred in India
phiran	traditional Kashmiri outfit for women
raddiwala	scrap dealer
rickshawwala	driver of a light three-wheeled passenger vehicle
roti	a round flatbread native to the Indian subcontinent, made from stoneground wholemeal flour and water combined into a dough
sindhi	an Indo-Aryan ethno-linguistic group
shuddhi	purification, cleansing and freedom from defilement
thali	an Indian-style meal with various dishes served on a platter
vat purnima	a celebration observed by married women in India
virat roop	strong and majestic form
yogis	practitioners of yoga
zamindar	a landowner, especially one who leases his land to tenant farmers

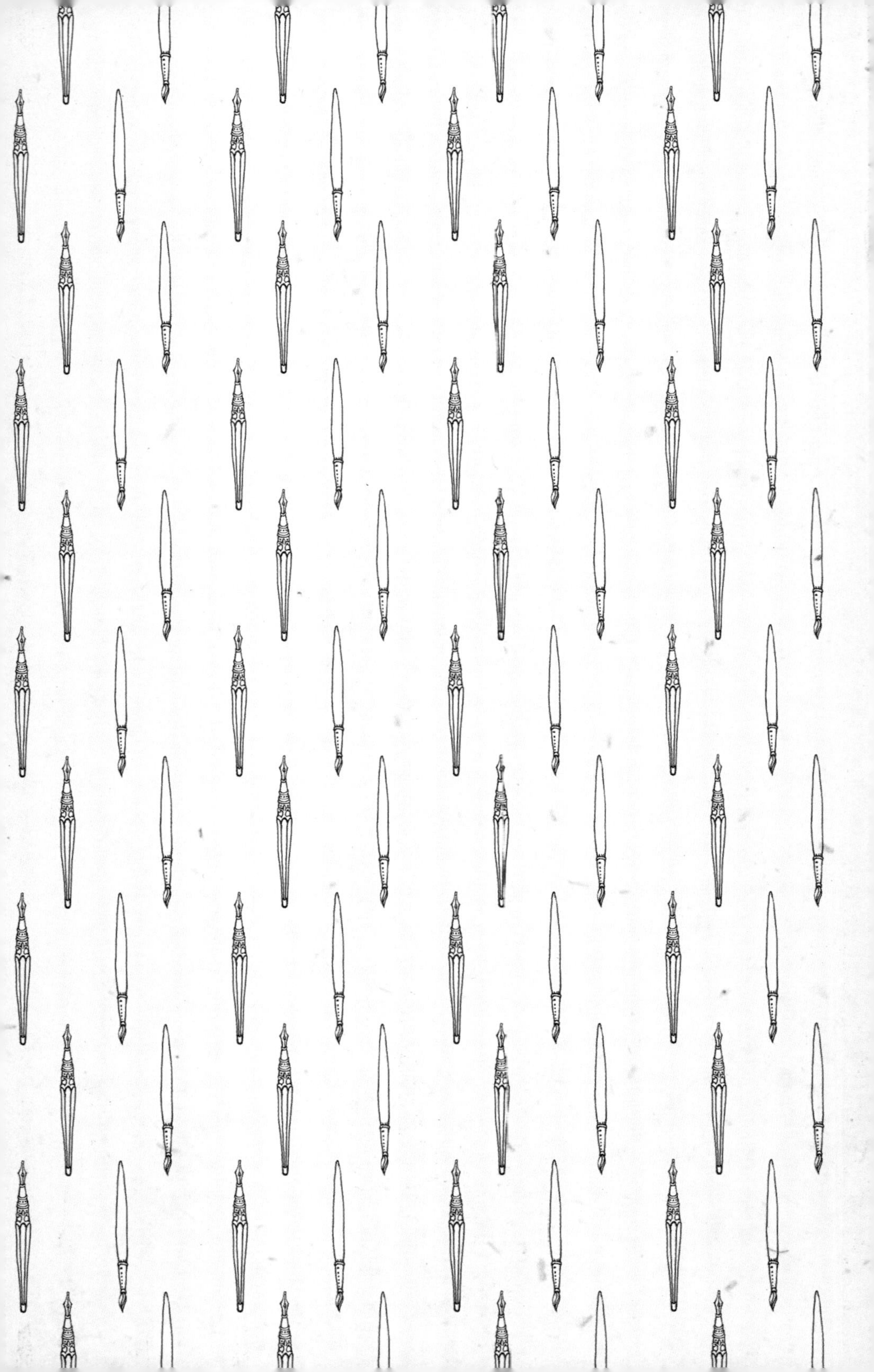